FOR THE
LEAST
of
THESE

REFLECTIONS OF A PRISON LIBRARIAN

FRED A. WINN

Ark House Press
arkhousepress.com

Unless otherwise stated, all Scriptures are taken from the New Hendrickson Parallel Bible which includes: King James; New King James; NIV; New Living Translation 2nd Edition. All rights reserved.

Some names and identifying details have been changed to protect the privacy of individuals.

Cataloguing in Publication Data:
Title: For The Least Of These
ISBN: 978-0-6453370-3-7 (pbk)
Subjects: Memoirs; Christian Living; California prisons; American Evangelicals; Civil Rights Struggles; African American Churches; California Inmate Politics; Urban Life; Origin of Pro-Life Movement;
Other Authors/Contributors: Winn, Fred

Design by initiateagency.com
Original cover photograph attributed to: (1915) Convicts Leased to Harvest Timber. Florida United States of America, 1915. [Place of Publication Not Identified: Publisher Not Identified] [Photograph] Retrieved from the Library of Congress, https://www.loc.gov/item/2021669926/.

To the Family of Green and Hannah Allen Winn

Matthew 25:41-46,

"Then shall He say also unto them on the left hand 'Depart from Me, ye cursed, into everlasting fire, prepared for the devil and his angels: For I was hungry, and you gave me no food: I was thirsty, and you gave Me no drink: I was a stranger, and you did not take Me in, naked and you did not clothe Me, sick and in prison, and you did not visit Me. Then they also will answer Him, saying, 'Lord, when did we see You hungry or thirsty or a stranger or naked or sick or in prison, and did not minister to you?' Then He will answer them, saying, 'Assuredly, I say to you, in as much as you did not do it to one of the least of these, you did not do it to Me'. "And these will go away into everlasting punishment, but the righteous into eternal life."

Contents

Introduction

A long white line runs down the center of Soledad State Prison's main corridor. I used to walk this line every day. Each working day I entered an alien world to interact with California's criminal element.

My name is Fred Winn, aka Mr. Allen. I was employed by the California Department of Corrections for nearly 25 years.

I grew up in the San Francisco Bay Area and attended an African American Church in Berkeley, California. As a youth I was not aware of the term, 'African American Church'. I just thought of it as church. My family (including extended family members) spent several hours there each Sunday and attended services during the week. Although I still hold fast to the teachings of my youth, I do not identify as an evangelical.

I lived in the East Bay for the first three decades of my life. Following the deaths of my parents, I accepted a position as Senior Librarian with the California Department of Corrections. I moved from the San Francisco Bay Area to Monterey County. I was in my early thirties.

At the time of this move, a first-class postage stamp cost 22 cents, and the movie *Back to the Future* was a mega-hit. A soft drink company changed the recipe for its flagship soft drink; however, the reaction was so adverse that it returned the original product to the market within months.

During my career in corrections, I held several positions at two separate prisons—the Correctional Training Facility and the Salinas Valley

State Prison - both situated in Monterey County. The prisons are located on US Route 101, five miles north of Soledad, California. Farmers in the Salinas Valley area provide vegetables to homes all over the country. During the 1970s, the Correctional Training Facility received significant media attention due to several inmates known as the *Soledad Brothers*.

The central facility housed 1,000 inmates, with a thousand different stories about the lack of justice resulting in their incarceration - some of these stories were even true. When combined with the reasons my colleagues gave for working in this alien environment, one gets even more stories. I would know. I was the law librarian and had stories of my own.

As a law librarian, I was responsible for maintaining the court-mandated law collection, the college and general collections for the inmate population. Most of the inmates had minimal library experience before coming to prison. I found it professionally rewarding to provide much-needed services for this underserved group.

Before entering the prison for the first time, I thought I would encounter an atmosphere of despair. I expected to find a place housing the downhearted, the heavy laden, the poor in spirit, and a community of men with disappointment as their sole companion. A place where dreams turned into nightmares and aspirations ceased to exist. I soon found that was not always the case. I often found much laughter and people full of hope.

Most inmates confined within California's criminal justice system are men and women of color. Almost all inmates, including White inmates, come from challenging sectors of society. This mass incarceration of poor people does not appear to concern many members of the evangelical community. Their attitude appears to be *this is just the way of the world, and/or poor people along with members of the minority population belong behind bars.*

Some members of the evangelical community deny that enslaved Africans created enormous wealth for the country while receiving little in return when every page of United States history tells a different story. Ten out of the first twelve presidents were slavers. Many evangelicals cannot acknowledge that the history of Black Americans is one of intense persecution, and political, social, and economic marginalization. To be fair, evangelicals are far from being the only ones with this viewpoint. Nazis, White supremacist, Ku Klux Klan members to name a few express similar views. However, I believe that all members of Christian Organizations claiming to be followers of Jesus Christ, should be held to a higher standard.

While antisemitism comprised the core of Nazi ideology, Black people and others living in Germany during this period also suffered greatly. They faced forced labor camps, sterilization, medical experimentation, and murder.

Germany dealt with its horrific past by highlighting the deeds of the evildoers, not building statues honoring them. What would life be like in present-day Germany for Blacks, members of the Jewish community, and others if monuments to Nazi leaders were in public places? Suppose towns, bridges, and buildings were to bear the names of Nazi generals? Suppose members of these persecuted communities had to navigate streets named after Hitler or enter courtrooms seeking justice with images of the Fuhrer all over the building. Fortunately, German citizens do not have to contend with such madness, unlike African Americans.

Yet, many members of the Christian right join those claiming that removing Confederate symbols is equal to attempts to erase or cancel history. At the same time, many members of this same group support laws that ban the actual teaching of history because they claim to find it *uncomfortable*. This group appears unconcerned about the 'feelings' of nonwhites. Black people arriving as members of the enslaved class have been uncomfortable on these shores since 1619.

It is difficult for some to view such persons as part of the body of Christ when they hold such questionable views on the *Least of These*. Instead of standing with those on the side of freedom, they choose to identify with those honoring murderers, enslavers, kidnappers, traitors, and rapists. By so doing, they are choosing evil over good, ignorance over knowledge, lies over truth, and mythology over actual events.

Many people in these evangelical groups join those unable to utter *Black Lives Matter* and instead say, '*All Lives Matter*.' *Despite my research, I have been unable to determine when all lives mattered equally in this country. The fact that these groups support banning teaching history but retaining Confederate symbols suggests that they do not believe all lives matter equally.*

When members of the group feel uncomfortable with certain portions of United States history, they support laws to prevent such discussions in classrooms. When Black people view Confederate symbols as figures of oppression, causing physical discomfort, the response is to *get over it*. In my view, the Christian church in America has not defended nor spoken up for the marginalized groups among us as aggressively as it should. All too often, the church is on the side of the oppressor instead of the oppressed.

These are a few of the issues raised in this book.

I retained the post of law librarian for nine years or so. From a professional perspective, this period was enriching and deeply fulfilling. I like to think I played a small part in helping some of the inmates along the road to achieving or at least recognizing their potential. I also tried to help prisoners enhance their quality of life by exposing them to new tools, ideas, and in some cases, a different perspective on which to view life experiences.

This book offers readers a glimpse of life behind bars and, in some cases, chronicling events leading to incarceration. The stories are based on real inmates. The names and some events have been altered to protect their identity. It also shares some thoughts on the Christian community's response to pressing social issues in the past and present day.

CHAPTER 1

The Beginning

This section is in part my story and the period of adjustments one makes to a new job and environment. The other part of the story touches on inmate peer pressure, and the degree inmate groups can influence their peers. Inmates often face two separate disciplinary systems, the Official Department of Corrections disciplinary system and the inmate disciplinary system. The inmate hierarchy often administrated a second set of disciplinary rules and procedures. In these cases, inmates could face disciplinary actions by both systems for the same offense. These formal and informal systems provided me with a new appreciation of the term *double jeopardy*.

Within weeks, I discovered prisons were full of wrongly convicted, innocent individuals. I stumbled upon this knowledge through conversations with several inmates. They all claimed to be innocent - or at least most so claimed - and at the same time, the guilty parties ran free to continue a life of crime. In other words, they were set up, and most were 'pencil whipped' by members of the public safety communities. At least that was their story!

I soon found these setups continued behind the prison walls when an inmate came into the library seeking information to appeal a disciplinary report after testing positive for an illegal substance. I was surprised, for he was a pious, profoundly religious man, even though he did not belong to a group recognized by any of the major world religions.

The only people who considered the group religious were its faithful members. Some referred to the group as a bunch of 'nuts', while others referred to it as a 'cult'. Nevertheless, the 'cult' required members to adhere to strict rules and regulations. Failure to do so could result in excruciating painful disciplinary action from the cult leadership. These rules included abstaining from alcohol, tobacco products, and illegal drugs.

The inmate explained that it was not his fault. He saw some of his neighborhood friends hanging out on the prison yard, not members of his religious group. They appeared to be having a good time, so he decided to join the group. His friends were passing a cigarette around; it reached him. He inquired as to the contents of the cigarette; someone said tobacco. After a quick look around and not seeing any religious sect members, he decided to partake. After all, all of us fall short. He took a hit and noticed the smoke had a strange taste and smell. He again inquired about the contents of the cigarette, and the answer was the same, tobacco. His friends suggested the reason for his confusion was the fact that he had not smoked anything since joining those 'lunatics'. He accepted this explanation and continued to smoke.

This behavior - cigarette passing, and a particular smell combined with loud laughter - attracted the attention of a correctional officer. Thus, a failed drug test was followed by a disciplinary report.

This encounter turned into a learning experience for the inmate. He discovered that one should not hang out with people possessed by demons.

"Demons?" I asked.

"Yeah, they all had demons causing them to lie. Who knows how many other evil spirits they had in them? All they did was tell lies."

"What about vampires?" I joked.

But the inmate did not get the joke. He thought I was serious and responded as such.

The inmate described how vampires were even worse. They were needy, greedy, and would suck the lifeblood out of a person. It turns out he was referring to one-sided friendships—people who took far more than they ever gave and were always in need of a bit of help. Unfortunately, they were never around or lacked the necessary resources, or just made excuses when you needed a favor.

However, this group was different from backstabbers, who smile in one's face while stabbing the person in the back. Therefore, these betrayers are the lowest of the low. In the end, we both agreed one should avoid those who are possessed by demons, vampires, or those who stabbed others in the back.

POSTSCRIPT:

In this case, the disciplinary action from the cult was light. The inmate received a black eye and a couple of other bruises. To my knowledge, he remained committed to the organization and its value system.

About 10 years before this incident, I was in the company of two of my father's brothers, watching a gangster movie on television. When one of the characters wanted to leave or quit the organization, he was told to talk to the boss. After explaining his reasons for wanting to leave the group, the boss gave a signal, and the guy wanting to leave got shot. My oldest uncle turned to me and warned, "Nephew, whatever you do, don't join a group where they don't let you quit." We all laughed with my uncle. I have often thought about that and concluded that it might be good to avoid groups that administer physical punishments for violating its rules.

CHAPTER 2

The search for an inmate worker

O *ne of the many challenges of corrections employment is finding hon-est, reliable inmate workers. This story is about the search for such a worker—a library clerk. I was fortunate to have had several reliable workers and volunteers over the years. However, the beginning months were rough going.*

People often ask me what it was like working amongst criminals. The answer to that question is simple. I chose not to look at them as criminals. One of my inmate workers offered me sound advice during my first month at Soledad State Prison.

The inmate worker said, "Mr. Allen, you should be careful as many of these guys are here for murder, robbery, kidnapping, and other seri-ous crimes. I am not a dangerous man. I got popped for selling a little cocaine. That's it. It would help if you went to the office where all the prisoner files are. That way, you will know what's up."

A few weeks later, a clerk position became available in the prison's Protective Custody Unit. This unit had several clerk positions available to inmates. This unit's policy stated that an inmate should be selected for a position based on an expression of interest. My job was to find a suitable inmate for the clerk position. There are two separate lockup units in the prison, Protective Custody Unit and the Administrative Segregation Unit.

In the Administrative Segregation Unit, most inmates are placed in this unit, pending completion of the disciplinary process, while others are pending transfer to another prison. The inmates remain in their assigned cells for 23 out of 24 hours, and when they leave their cells, they are under direct escort and placed in restraint gear.

In the Protective Custody Unit, the inmates are deemed unsuitable for assimilation within the general inmate population, often for safety reasons. The inmates tend to remain in their housing units but not their cells.

To process the selection of a clerk, I obtained a list of names from the Protective Custody Unit, but only for those inmates who expressed an interest in a clerk position in the library. As an inmate's file was confidential, I went to the records office. I presented the list of names to the secretary who retrieved the files. As I couldn't take them out of the records office, I sat down at an empty desk to review them.

The first applicant had a grade point level of 11.3 with an insignificant disciplinary history. So far, so good. The guy had skills and was not prone to making trouble. I noted that before his incarceration, he was in the closet regarding his sexual orientation. Not only did he not come out to family and friends, but he was also unable to admit his sexual preference to himself. When he could no longer control his urges, he would travel to a nearby city to a specific park. Here he would find other men who met for anonymous consensual same-sex encounters and find a partner. Upon completion of the sex act, he would kill the partner for reasons known only to those with extensive psychological training. On the night of his arrest, the local police department was conducting an unrelated undercover operation in the park and responded to the victim's screams. As I crossed his name from my list, I recall thinking, *this guy belongs in the nuthouse.*

The second applicant had previously told me he was a genius with a very high IQ. Perhaps I was expecting too much. Maybe I thought I would be reading the story of a criminal genius that would cause even the great Sherlock Holmes to stumble. As I read about a guy who befriended lonely men and women with assets, I realized this was not the case. He would enter their lives and perform acts of kindness, gaining their trust. At some point, the acts of kindness would cease, and the lucky ones would return home to an empty house. The unlucky ones were murdered and then dismembered. However, he claimed that the dismemberment was not a by-product of insanity but to prevent authorities from identifying the remains. Maybe he should have also pulled their teeth, as the police used dental charts for identification. Not only was he not a genius, but he was a vile, immoral, depraved monster. So the search for a new clerk continued.

Years later, I had an interesting conversation with this inmate. He was upset due to an unfavorable response from the courts. Prior to this most recent ruling, he had - according to him, successfully appealed two of his three life sentences but fell short on this most recent legal effort. In the justice system, one life sentence is all it takes to keep one in prison for life. This inmate felt no one ever does more than one life sentence, so the other victories were hollow. He failed to find comfort in only having one life sentence to serve. He rejected my arguments that sometimes hollow victories can be significant, much like small pleasures. Sometimes it is all one has. Besides, the issues raised in his successful appeals may be of assistance to others. But he, much like many others, only thought of himself. According to rumors, he later submitted a request for a pardon to the Governor's Office, resulting in laughter being heard throughout the building when the request was received.

The third applicant's file told the story of an equally cruel, morally flawed man who had been a nurse. For reasons that were not clear, he bounced from one job to another until landing a nursing position at a hospital in the California Central Valley. Things were going well until someone noticed two things. When several suspicious deaths occurred, he was either on duty or had left within minutes of each death. An investigation into his previous employment revealed other suspicious deaths, with authorities questioning him on these matters. He was eventually arrested and found guilty of committing four murders, although more than that had occurred. He admitted to performing acts of kindness by putting patients out of their misery and conceded that none of the victims requested his help to end their suffering. He said he took pity on them when he saw the mental, emotional, or physical anguish they suffered. He also said ending their suffering was the only decent thing to do. The court disagreed and sentenced him to a long prison term. Another nut! The search continued.

The fourth applicant's file contained the story of a man in a landscaping business who found a creative way to manage labor costs. He would hire day laborers, pay them daily for a day or two as a trial period, and then offer full-time employment. This approach resulted in biweekly pay instead of daily pay. A day or two before the first biweekly check, the landscaper, posing as a loyal, patriotic citizen, would contact the Immigration and Naturalization Service with information about illegal aliens. The workers would be arrested and deported, with the landscaper pocketing the wages. (The landscaper also faced Federal charges.) This form of deceit is not a nice thing for anyone to do. The workers had families to feed, rent to pay, and so on, and were entitled to their pay. Some would argue they should have come into this country legally. However, I believe no one is entitled to free labor, not this landscaper or those who enslaved Africans for generations. However, I do understand the need for strong immigration laws. The Indigenous people of this continent welcomed newcomers from Europe, even helping them survive their first harsh winters. *We all know how this worked out for the Native Americans.*

The fifth applicant's file was about a man who lacked impulse control and had other issues. He and his partner in crime were in the process of robbing a liquor store when they heard police sirens approaching. They reached their car and fled the scene with the loot, with the police soon in hot pursuit. The passenger, aware of an alley entrance several feet away that offered a reasonable chance to escape, told the driver to turn at the corner. The driver sped past the alley and turned at the next traffic light. The passenger became so enraged at this missed opportunity he shot the driver while the car was traveling 60 miles per hour in a 30 miles per hour zone. The driver's concentration began to wane, perhaps due to pain or maybe his body going into shock. The driver lost control of the vehicle, and within hours both were in the county hospital under police guard. The driver later claimed he had committed the crime under duress, offering as proof the fact that his partner shot him. The partner countered this claim, and they both went to prison. I assume they were both unfamiliar with the concept of honor among thieves.

I decided to stop reviewing the inmate files as they contained too much information. Instead, I chose to enter the prison gates each day, pretending I was arriving at a church social for the untoward. A gathering where the inmates were guilty of minor infractions like leaving church early or singing too loud in the choir. I must admit that a few incidents put this approach into question, but it often worked.

In the prison world, respect amongst inmates was paramount. Those inmates who gave respect most often received it. To disrespect someone—or in prison language popular during this period *front someone-off* - could result in severe injury or worse.

As it happened, I seldom knew what crimes had been committed by the inmate workers and library users. I simply attempted to treat them as I wanted others to treat me. I was not always successful, but I made a genuine effort for 25 years.

POSTSCRIPT:

On the drive home later that day I was reminded of the biblical story found in the 18th Chapter of Genesis. God has plans to destroy a city but makes an agreement with Abraham not to do so, if Abraham can find 50 righteous people living there. Abraham knows it would be a challenge to find that many righteous people there, so he pleads with God, and God eventually agrees that if Abraham could find 10 righteous people living there, He will spare the city. The bottom line: the city got destroyed.

CHAPTER 3

The education of inmate Oliver

E *ducation is key to get a job or a better job and demonstrates a certain amount of skill and determination in a person. This story is about an inmate who learned to read and write while incarcerated and the impact on his life and his family's life. It is also the story about the power of one person touching and positively influencing the lives of several people.*

Oliver's story is like countless other inmates I met over the years. It is the story of accepting responsibility, making positive changes, and discounting the opinion of peers. The impact of one teacher on the life of Oliver and his family is profound. The teacher will never meet these family members and may never know the positive effects.

Upon entering the correctional and detention facilities (a prison), each inmate undergoes a battery of tests to determine their reading level. Oliver's level was equivalent to a lower elementary level, 1st through 3rd grade. All scores below the 6th grade level required placement in the prison's education department at the appropriate academic level. Oliver's test scores resulted in a mandatory Adult Basic Education I placement.

Oliver was deeply disappointed. He did not want to sit in a classroom listening to a boring teacher all day. Oliver just wanted an assignment with pay and the opportunity to steal items to supplement the meager income he would receive. Many job assignments did not include a salary, and in those cases, one had to rely totally on thievery to get by.

Oliver had limited interest in school before he was incarcerated and even less now. He was not against education for others, it was just not for him, and he did not understand why he was required to attend. He could appreciate the necessity of school if he wanted to be a lawyer, brain surgeon, or something requiring special training. But his ambitions lie in other areas, like getting high in the morning and drunk at night.

Now that he was in prison, he had to lower his expectations, not raise them. Oliver's current goals were to hang out with his *homeboys* while they looked for mischief and to have enough money to go to the canteen. None of his friends were interested in school either. He explained that it was a *bird of the feather* kind of thing.

Oliver explained to the correctional counselor that education was not an option he would consider. If assigned, he would refuse to go. The counselor simply told him it was not a problem, but he could sit in his cell 22 hours a day, seven days a week. In addition, the counselor also said that if he changed his mind, he could send a kite (note).

The correctional counselor knew some things Oliver had yet to discover. He placed himself on *hard C status* by refusing to program. The *hard C* status inmates were allowed out of their cells for breakfast - where they also received a box lunch - and returned to their cells until the evening meal. After the evening meal, they returned to their cells and remained until breakfast the next day. They were allowed yard time one afternoon per week and canteen privileges every six months.

Within a day or two, this routine got old. Oliver sent a kite to his counselor, requesting placement on the academic waiting list. The counselor responded with a kite advising him to *sit tight and stay out of trouble, and the captain would consider his request in a month or two.* In response to Oliver's next kite, the counselor further explained that the captain was a very busy man with over 350 inmates under his supervision. A person with that much responsibility could not drop everything to attend to minor concerns. In addition, the captain had just approved Oliver's placement on *hard C* status.

Oliver's workgroup eventually changed from *C* to *B* with placement on the academic waiting list. With this change, life got better for Oliver. He received yard privileges several times per week, canteen privileges once per quarter, and day room activities a couple of times a week. He could also place collect phone calls home once a week or so during day room activities.

When he received an academic assignment, life got even better. He left his cell for school every day and had yard or dayroom privileges each evening. He also had more opportunities to call home, of which he took full advantage.

After a couple of weeks of telephone calls, his mother suggested limiting the expensive collect calls to once per month and writing letters instead. Oliver agreed to this. However, it proved more difficult than anyone imagined and presented a three-fold challenge. The letters were arduous to write, impossible to be delivered, and difficult for the family to decipher.

Instead of daydreaming the next day in class, Oliver drafted a letter to his family. After a day or two of work, he addressed an envelope and gave both to his housing officer for mailing.

A week after posting, Oliver called home and found his family had not received his letter. Two weeks later, his letter was returned from the post office with a red stamp on the front. He tried to talk to the correctional officer that had handed him the letter. Oliver attempted to return the letter to the officer explaining that his family was waiting for it. The correctional officer glanced at the letter with the red stamp and said the post office could not deliver his letter. Oliver demanded to know what made it undeliverable as the letter had the necessary postage.

The correctional officer glanced at it again and responded, *you must be 5150. This writing looks like the scratching of a chicken. I suggest you take the letter to your teacher. I am a correctional officer, not a babysitter.* The California Welfare and Institution Code Section *5150* deals with involuntary commitments to mental health institutions.

When Oliver went to the teacher to discuss the letter and the term *5150*, the teacher explained that the term *5150* was unfamiliar. The teacher understood the King's English, not slang. Not even American slang. After examining the envelope, the teacher asked Oliver a few questions. She asked questions because the city and street appeared to be misspelt, and she was unsure where his family lived. She explained to Oliver that the post office handles thousands of packages each hour. Employees do not have time to spend more than a few seconds on each item. Thus, one must write clearly.

Oliver explained that his family had recently moved and provided him with their new address over the phone. He also acknowledged that his spelling might be a little off. He told the teacher his family's new residence and then attempted to correct his spelling. The teacher sent him to the library to consult the zip code directory to determine if the dwelling was within the zip code Oliver provided. This discovery made Oliver aware that the library contained useful information.

The teacher adjusted his education program because each student was engaged in an independent study. After understanding that the post office could not decipher his writing, Oliver spent the next week working on his handwriting and printing skills to address this.

For the first time in years, Oliver took school seriously. He worked diligently and completed all assignments. Gold stars were his reward. It was the first education-related victory he could recall. Oliver viewed gold stars with disdain before receiving his first gold star (when class-mates received stars for their efforts). However, now he was on the receiving end, and success was sweet.

Before long, Oliver addressed an envelope the teacher approved as acceptable. He had not rewritten the contents of his original message, just the envelope directing the postal service to its new location. This time Oliver experienced partial success.

On his next call home, Oliver spent the entire time explaining the contents of his letter to his family. *It appears that postal employees were not the only ones lacking deciphering skills.* Nevertheless, Oliver returned to school the next day with a renewed determination to improve his communication skills. Several years and many gold stars later, Oliver acquired the necessary credits for high school graduation. He then entered and completed the vocational landscaping program.

Along the way, he started writing long letters to his family that the post office delivered, and his family could read. He sent his completed schoolwork, with gold stars, home to his children and requested copies of their schoolwork in return. At first, Oliver encouraged and later demanded they apply themselves in school. He asked for books - some-times via the interlibrary loan system - the same books as his children were assigned to share thoughts. Oliver insisted his children visit their local library and obtain library cards. He also encouraged their mother to take an active interest in their academic progress and meet with their teachers.

As noted, Oliver eventually graduated from high school and com-pleted the vocational landscaping program. He also completed the requirements for a degree in general education from the local commu-nity college offered through the prison education program.

Oliver eventually found a world beyond gangs and drugs. One teacher had a significant impact on Oliver and his children. This teacher provided the spark igniting his interest in learning, thus increasing his skill level putting him on the path to becoming a productive member of society.

This same teacher had 23 other students. All these students did not experience success at this level, although most reached the required state-mandated 6th-grade reading level. Oliver's educational achievements made the world more accessible. Oliver's educational experience reflects the 'power of one.' One person had a profound impact on the life of Oliver and his family.

POSTSCRIPT:

Many argue that public funds are wasted on inmate education. They oppose exposing inmates to music and the arts as well as vocational training. However, I believe that it is important to consider that most inmates are eventually released from prison back into the community. It is my view that it is in the best interest of society for inmates to leave prison with a reasonable chance of leading a productive, law-abiding life.

CHAPTER 4

The case of the Black books

In the mid-1980s, the concept of multiculturalism within the book collection of an inmate library was not in vogue at Soledad State Prison. Ordering books by and about African Americans caused a great deal of concern in some circles. This story is about the first of several battles I had with an unknown adversary in the warehouse, whose name I never knew. The warehouse manager was a kind and helpful gentleman who directly brought issues to my attention, so I knew the manager was not the culprit. This story is also about the inner-working of the inmate communication system - one that I was completely unaware existed. I learned a valuable lesson from this experience - a lesson that I drew from many times over the years. The lesson was that inmates often know things are going to happen before they happen.

For most of the world, the working week starts on a Monday. For me, my working week started on a Sunday. I remember it was on a Tuesday; the emergency lockdown status had ended early that morning, resulting in numerous inmates requesting library services.

While some inmates without assignments that morning rushed to the prison yard for fresh air, others came to the library. Since the library did not open for 45 minutes, I sent everyone, except my clerks, to the *East Gate* to wait.

This morning, inmate Herrera, my valuable lead clerk, immediately approached me, stating he needed to discuss *a most urgent matter*. This tactic was *par for the course* with him. Herrera frequently found urgent matters requiring my immediate attention. They were issues that, upon examination, were urgent only to him. In hindsight, I did not give this issue the attention it deserved.

After completing my security checks and other housekeeping items, I invited Herrera into my office, closed the door, and asked him what was wrong. Herrera started by stating that urgent matters require immediate attention. *I got it. He was offended I made him wait.* I realized he could go on like this for a good 10 minutes. So, I cut him short by agreeing that urgent things required a higher priority than less critical things and asked if that was all.

The answer was no. Herrera continued that a vast conspiracy existed within the prison's underbelly to keep people of color *in their place*. I was currently in their crosshairs. He stated I was the first *gentleman of color* employed in the position I held. He further stated that people, both staff and inmates, found this situation unbearable. It was a problem that required fixing before I completed my probationary period. Once one completed probation, termination was more difficult but not impossible. Evil forces were stalking me, and I had to watch every step. This monologue was a bit much, even for him. He had my complete attention.

Herrera informed me that my supervisor would contact me at around 9:00 a.m. regarding a specific book order. However, there was no need for me to worry; he had my back. He handed me a sheet of paper containing *talking points* and said if I followed his advice, all would be well.

I was aware my supervisor, Mr. Bell, would be in a budget meeting for most of the day, and the two of us did not have an appointment scheduled. I graciously thanked Herrera for the heads-up and promptly disregarded his advice. I should have left it at that but chose not to.

Instead, I asked him about his mental health and if he was still on psychiatric medications. His face fell as he admitted to being in the mental health program and quickly said he was not *5150*. Since we established that he was on medication, I asked him if he was taking his medication, to which he responded yes. However, when I asked if he took his medication today, he responded no. Before I could ask if he was on evening medications, he said yes, and had taken his medication last night and intended to comply with tonight's medication requirement.

Furthermore, he did not understand the need for this line of questioning. He felt there always existed a conspiracy in this country to undermine the progress of people of color. In addition, he thought anyone with a basic knowledge of the history of the United States would be aware of this fact, that is, unless they are stupid. *I wondered if that last statement was referring to me.*

Before I could ask, he continued and said one did not have to examine American history in its entirety. One only had to pick a decade, any decade, and evidence of the conspiracy would leap off the pages for those with eyes to see.

At this point, the Emergency Alarm System activated. I escorted Herrera out of the office, locked it, and performed my regular emergency-related duties.

As it turned out, Herrera was wrong on two counts. I received a visit, not a phone call, and it came around 11:00 a.m., not 9:00 a.m. I remember the East Corridor officer opening the library door to admit Mr. Freeman. Mr. Freeman informed me that Mr. Bell wanted to see me.

We exchanged keys - keys play a critical role in prisons - so I could roam around at will in the education wing, and he could do likewise in the library.

Mr. Freeman remained in the library to supervise the inmates while I met with Mr. Bell. The purpose of my meeting was unknown to me; the conversation with inmate Herrera did not enter my mind.

As I arrived at Mr. Bell's office, his secretary appeared somewhat distant as she said to go on in, as he was expecting me. As soon as I walked in, Mr. Bell seemed agitated. He asked about my weekend, hoping it was enjoyable, and then got to the point. The purpose of this meeting was in regards to a shipment of "Black" books that had arrived at the warehouse, around 2,000 dollars' worth. *My annual budget was about 14,000 dollars.*

Now it was my turn to become agitated. "What?" I shouted as I half leapt out of my chair. I was in shock.

What in the world was going on? Was I in a bad dream? How could Herrera possess information regarding future events? Was my clerk psychic? Are psychics even real?

Although Herrera often laid claims to various skills, he had yet to claim supernatural powers. I was aware that prison could be weird. Down was up, and up was down. For example, to refer to someone as *nice* was considered an insult. But this future thing! As inmates would often ask, "What's up with that?"

I suddenly noticed Mr. Bell's countenance had changed. He had a strange look on his face and was speaking in a low, soothing voice. I pushed the psychic question out of my mind and focused on what my supervisor was saying.

He said that no one was questioning my judgment. On the contrary, everyone talks about how professional I am.

I wondered what he was talking about now. Then it dawned on me. He had misinterpreted the source of my agitation. He assumed he was the source. Before his very eyes, I had changed from a *mild-mannered gentleman of color* to an *angry Black man*. This impression will never do. I could hear him in the Warden's Office saying, *By the way, we must get rid of that guy. He is one of those militants. Very touchy! I can't even talk to him.* While I was not planning to work there forever, my plans did not include leaving soon.

I eased back into my seat and spoke slowly in a calm voice as I said, "Well, you may not be questioning my judgment, but it sounds like someone is."

I could see him relax. I suddenly remembered inmate Herrera's *talking points*. I reached into the empty pocket of my sports jacket before remembering that I had left his notes in my desk drawer. I also remembered questioning Herrera's mental health rather than taking a moment to at least glance at them.

I thought of dashing out to retrieve his notes for a few seconds but decided against doing so. What excuse could I use for leaving? *Give me a moment to seek advice from an inmate.* No, that would not work. Besides, for all I knew, his notes might have contained the ravings of a lunatic. Although he was knowledgeable, he occasionally voiced conspiracy theories. As to his claim of not being *5150*, I only had his word for it; he was on medication after all. No, I was on my own!

I asked in a calm voice, "What exactly is a Black book? I assume you are talking about each title's contents or subject matter and not the color of the cover." He agreed. I continued, "So a book that deals with the contributions of, say, Asian Americans would be an Asian book, and a book about Hispanic Americans would be a Hispanic book. Likewise, a book that addresses the contributions of Black Americans would be a Black book, correct?"

Yes, he agreed. He also smiled. At that point, I decided to mix things up a bit. I continued, "So a book that has only White people in it would be a White book, correct?"

His smile disappeared. I pretended to be confused and asked for an explanation. "No. I mean, not necessarily. They could be just books," he explained.

For a brief second, he looked at me as if he thought I was crazy but quickly pulled himself together and offered to discuss these issues soon, just not today. Today, he was required to write a memo to the Warden regarding this purchase order and urgently needed my assistance.

I suggested he tell the Warden that the books in question were on American history, not Black American history but American history period. I further explained that the market for 'Black books' exists because this information is not included in American history or in 'White books'.

I asked which titles were considered offensive. Mr. Bell glanced at his notes, which appeared to be a copy of the purchase order, and replied, "He did not say. Who is Matthew Henson?"

I advised Mr. Bell that Henson was the first recorded non-Indigenous person to reach the North Pole. Or you can say Henson and not Perry should be the person in history books credited with getting to the North Pole first.

"What?" shouted Mr. Bell in disbelief.

I explained that Henson, an experienced explorer of the region, was a member of Perry's party. The area was full of danger, including home to hostile bears and other environmental threats. As the only Black guy in the group, Henson, was attached to a long rope and sent ahead.

Perry's party communicated via the rope. Henson would pull on the rope to signal that it was safe to proceed. That is how Henson arrived at the Pole ahead of Perry and the others. Upon returning from the Pole, Henson was under the impression he would be in demand as a speaker based on his North Pole experiences. Perry, however, downplayed Henson's role suggesting Henson did little more than carry their bags.

On his deathbed, Perry admitted that Henson's navigation skills played an essential role in reaching the North Pole safely.

Mr. Bell looked unconvinced and asked, "What about Charles Drew?"

I responded, "Doctor Drew was not only a physician but also a talented medical researcher. His research and subsequent breakthrough in blood transfusion and blood storage saved thousands of Allied Soldiers' lives. But guess how he died?"

"How?" asked Mr. Bell.

"He had an accident, lost a great deal of blood, and was rushed to the nearest hospital. Unfortunately, that hospital's policy did not allow *people of color* admittance or even treatment. Those transporting him explained that although he was *colored,* he was an extraordinary person responsible for incredible advances in the medical field. These advances even saved the lives of White people. Surely, they could make an exception in this case. Unfortunately for Doctor Drew, his family, and the entire human race, this facility's high (or low) standards did not allow treatment of certain people regardless of their accomplishments. His medical contributions saved countless other lives, but not his own. My supervisor looked unconvinced.

"Who is Percy Julian?" asked Mr. Bell.

I responded that Julian was a research chemist who overcame incredible odds to obtain an education, including going overseas to study due to a lack of educational opportunities for African Americans. Julian received over 100 chemical patents, and his work laid the foundation for, among other things, birth control pills.

Mr. Bell looked at the list again and asked, "What about the *Whoreson* book?"

I explained that a well-known writer of urban fiction, Donald Goines, was the author of that title. Goines' books, written for an urban audience, were often referred to as street fiction, thus the title. The tone of this genre focused on the negative aspects of inner-city life, including profanity, crime, sex, violence, and often featured situations many inmates would find familiar. In Goines' novels, crime never pays. The villain dies during a criminal act or is apprehended by authorities and sent to prison for many years. The lessons are clear, and I believe our clientele needs to hear the message that crime never pays.

Mr. Bell went silent. After a few seconds, he stated that the person reporting this incident was not White. "This is not about race. The person bringing this issue to the Warden's attention said he has worked in the warehouse for 15 years. The librarians had never ordered Black books. He called it an outrage."

"Well, that is one thing we can agree on," I replied.

"Huh? What is that?" asked Mr. Bell.

"The outrage part," I replied.

Mr. Bell was confused, and I attempted to explain. "I am willing to bet that Black inmates were confined in this prison 15 years ago."

Mr. Bell conceded that point. He acknowledged that Black inmates were confined at Soledad State Prison when he arrived over two decades ago. I knew that. Brothers are always the first to be arrested and shipped off to incarceration.

I continued. "About 35% of the inmate population is Black, 35% Hispanic, 10% other, and 20% White. Correct?"

Mr. Bell agreed.

I continued to argue that it was an *outrage* for 80% of the inmate population to only have White books to read since the prison doors opened. These were books of limited interest. The prison library lacked information about their culture, history, or contributions to the American story made by people looking like them. This lack of information is a disservice to everyone.

A careful reading of White books suggests this country's development resulted from the contribution of only one group, which is utterly inconsistent with historical facts. The first European settlers would not have survived their first harsh winters without the help of the Indigenous people of this continent.

I concluded by saying my intended goal was to develop a collection that reflected the interests and concerns of the entire inmate population, not just 20%.

Mr. Bell jumped up, beaming. "You are ordering books reflecting the needs of the inmate population. Great."

He had his answer for the Warden and ended the meeting. He rushed me out of his office.

I hurried back to the library, exchanged keys with Mr. Freeman, bidding him farewell, and summoned Herrera into my office.

Herrera's first words to me were, "How did it go? Were the talking points helpful?"

"Forget all of that. How could you have known about the meeting?"

He was reluctant to answer because doing so might compromise the inmate code of ethics, something he was not at liberty to do.

I suspected he had other reasons for not sharing this information. Reasons that had to do with wanting me to believe he had extraordinary abilities, thus making himself more valuable to the overall library operations.

I reached into my desk drawer for an *Inmate Job Assignment Change* form. I informed Herrera that he would go from lead law clerk to junior janitor within 24 hours if he did not start talking immediately. Instead of consulting law books, he would be cleaning toilets. This gained his attention and he told me all he knew about the matter.

He explained that inmate Willis, a regular law library user, worked in the machine shop office and could access the institutional telephone system. In addition, Willis lived in the same housing unit as Herrera. Willis had a cousin, housed in a different facility, named Hawks, who worked in the warehouse. As a clerk, Hawks also had access to the telephone system. Hawks and Herrera had done time together, were acquainted, and were both jailhouse lawyers. While not friends, they were on friendly terms. Inmate politics require strict racial segregation among the general inmate population. The two cousins adhered to the racial line as the inmate culture demanded without embracing its racist philosophy. However, they saw people as individuals. Both enjoyed friendships with people from different backgrounds on the streets and, to the extent possible, behind bars.

Hawks was aware that the central library ordered law books beyond those mandated by the Department of Corrections. He eagerly awaited new law books and would review as many as possible while the books were still in the warehouse. In addition, he frequently ordered these titles via the interlibrary loan program. Likewise, Hawks was aware of the *Black book* matter but did not think anything improper about the purchase order. Furthermore, Hawks believed access to these law books far outweighed the Black book controversy.

Prison staff often talked openly in front of inmate workers, as if they were invisible, regarding a wide range of issues, such as in this case. Hawks overheard the staff discussing this purchase order. One angry staff member made plans to contact the Warden, while another suggested forgetting the entire matter. A third staff member suggested he call the Supervisor of Education instead. Finally, the outraged complainant vowed to reach out to the Warden and Education Supervisor first thing Monday morning to ensure the supervisor acted.

Hawks called Willis and explained the situation suggesting that Willis talk to the law clerk to give the librarian a heads up. After talking with Willis, Herrera developed his *talking points* to share with me.

I reviewed Herrera's notes during lunch and wished I had done so before the meeting. Herrera's *talking points* started with a professional opinion that *a library collection should always attempt to reflect the population it serves. Failure to do so is equivalent to dereliction.* He then launched into a passionate argument on the positive impact these titles could have on the inmate population, the operation of the prison, and the good people of the State of California.

When one hears only negative things about oneself and one's heritage, it can directly affect behavior. If a person believes he is a descendant of savages, one may use this information to engage in savagery. When a person of color learns of the contributions made by people of color and the odds they overcame, one may be inspired to achieve success.

Suppose one learns his subgroup made significant contributions to society. In that case, one may begin to view themselves positively; and others may also view members of this subgroup in a more positive light upon learning these things. If one discovers they may be a king's descendant, he may start acting like a prince. This behavior change begins in prison and continues upon release.

Herrera said that anyone advocating banning books containing truthful, yet uncomfortable information does not fully understand what America is all about. Nor do they understand the role of libraries in a modern free democratic society. Such woefully ignorant individuals should have zero input in formulating library policy.

Plumbers play an essential role in the prison's function and oversee all plumbing concerns. Likewise, education issues should be the purview of educators and library issues of librarians. Much like a medical doctor who would not consult the janitor regarding general surgery procedures, this librarian will not seek advice or warehouse approval regarding the library's book collection.

If the janitor wants to dispense medical advice, let him first go to and complete medical school. Likewise, let the warehouse worker go to and graduate from library school before attempting to dictate direction to me in my professional field.

Herrera ended on a personal note. *Remember, Mr. Allen, you are the first man of color in this position. Your employment in this position is their primary concern. Some people would like to get rid of you. Remember, history is on your side. Stay Strong.*

I had to admit his *talking points* would have been helpful in the meeting with Mr. Bell. After that incident, I vowed to pay close attention to Herrera if he ever talked about things that would take place in the future.

Postscript:

The wisest man that ever lived wrote, " There is nothing new under the Sun." While contributions to the American Story by people of color were often excluded from mainstream history books during this period, winds of change were blowing. Historical accounts began including contributions made by all Americans. However within the past year, the winds of change began blowing again, this time in the opposite direction with many states passing laws requiring school districts to refrain from including certain 'uncomfortable subjects' from the curriculum.

I was caught off guard over the issue of the Black books and the inmate grapevine.

My warehouse adversary returned several months later—or maybe it was a different person. By the time the next book controversy greeted me, *the previous education administrator had retired.* In any event, I was a seasoned employee and was not as surprised. I had come to expect opposition and bureaucratic infighting.

CHAPTER 5

The Jailhouse Lawyer

A jailhouse lawyer is an inmate lacking formal legal training who offers legal advice to fellow inmates. Over the years, I interacted with many jailhouse lawyers—some were good, some very good, and others not so good. I sometimes observed staff members conversing with my inmate clerks. One staff member appeared to be seeking counsel regarding state divorce laws, because the inmate handed her a self-help divorce guide. This story is about a not-so-good jailhouse lawyer - thankfully I never directly observed him give legal advice to staff.

When one starts a new job, one is confronted by many things, including new people, environment, and culture. During my first few months at Soledad State Prison, I adjusted to all the above, including issues unique to prison employment, including keys, locks, gates, noise, politics, and even crime.

One issue a new employee faces concerns supervising inmate workers. During my first week, my mentor, Mr Kirk, provided background information on each inmate worker. His critique on *Billy the Kid* stood out and not just because of his name.

The *Kid* was the ultimate jailhouse lawyer. Due to both job openings and hard work, he soon became a law clerk after starting as a janitor. As a law clerk, he never met a potential client he could not defend, unsuccessfully, as it turns out. After reviewing a potential client's previous legal filing, the *Kid* would locate errors made by their attorney and offer to file an appeal to correct these issues and bring about justice. He did all of this for the modest price of a carton or two of cigarettes. He sold hope to the hopeless and sweet dreams to the dreamless.

According to Mr. Kirk, the *Kid* claimed to have worked on his own appeal for several months before receiving a disappointing response the week before. He had received a one-word response to his appeal, *DENIED*, stamped on the Court of Appeals' letterhead.

While the *Kid* was usually quite the social animal, often bragging and full of laughter, he had become withdrawn and very serious. A concerned Mr. Kirk called him into the office to determine if he – Mr. Kirk - should be aware of a problem. The *Kid* explained the court's response to his appeal and complained that the response did not contain the reason for their ruling *like they do in the law books.*

Because Mr. Kirk was a kind and compassionate man, but primarily because he was curious, he offered to review the appeal and attempt to determine the reason behind the court's ruling. Mr. Kirk was not sure his efforts would be successful. After all, he lacked legal training, and the *Kid* had worked on his appeal for almost a year. However, Mr. Kirk claimed he found the answer in two minutes.

"Two minutes?" I asked.

"Make that less than two minutes," he said.

"How?"

"Well, I never read his writ to the Appeals Courts, but since he claimed his appeal was based on improper jury instructions, I decided to start my review there."

"What did you find?"

"Nada, zip. The judge failed to issue any instructions to the jury. At least, I assume he did not. I never got around to reading the transcripts."

"Well, the lack of proper instructions should be grounds for a successful appeal."

Mr. Kirk smiled. "Well, not always, or at least not in this case. The beginning papers of his trial proceeding indicated he had a bench trial. Thus, there was no jury for the judge to issue instructions. As far as I could tell from his conversation, the *Kid* slapped several different appeals together, included a few pages from the *Prisoner's Handbook*, and shipped it off to the court."

"So, you mean he was in court and never noticed that the jury box was empty?"

"Who knows. I never asked."

"What did you tell him?"

"I told him what he wanted to hear."

"Which was?"

"It was not his fault."

"Wait, you mean it was not his fault that he filed an appeal regarding instructions to the jury when he did not have a jury trial?"

"Yea."

"Whose fault, was it?"

"I told him it was society's fault."

"What! How was that society's fault?" I asked.

I explained that if society had made school more interesting, he might have completed school instead of dropping out. Instead, he left junior high for the juvenile hall, entered the youth authority and state prison. Some people veer into one of the military branches somewhere along these lines. However, he chose prison university, which offers a different career path with fewer options.

I also said that we all have gaps in our general knowledge, but there are some things one should know. Many subjects are not taught at prison university because it functions more like a vocational school for criminals. Prison also does not offer a liberal arts education. For example, one learns the earth revolves around the sun in school. If one is absent for that lesson, one could borrow another's notes, or another teacher in another class may cover this topic later. Other things are not in books, but one is penalized if not aware of them.

"Like not appealing jury instructions when you had a bench trial," I said.

"Exactly. There are things one picks up (or not) as we travel through life."

"So, he did not fail society; society failed him. Is that it?" I asked.

"Well, he was in pain, and I wanted to be helpful."

"Did your answer satisfy him?"

Kirk responded, "It seems so, but he has more pressing concerns. He has been filing appeals for his *clients*, and responses are starting to come back from the Courts. So far, rejection is the one thing they all have in common. Some of his clients are demanding the return of their cigarettes. Cigarettes he no longer has. Staff received information that one of his clients was not interested in having his cigarettes returned. This client exchanged cigarettes for hope and was unwilling to let go of the hope part. He plans to put a hit out and wants blood if his appeal is not granted."

When I returned to work the following day, the *Kid* had been unassigned from the library and confined to his cell pending placement in the Administrative Segregation Unit. He remained in the Administrative Segregation Unit until he transferred to an alternate level three prison. Staff determined that the *Kid* could not program safely at Soledad State Prison.

POSTSCRIPT:

The surgeon general of the United States was right. Cigarettes can be dangerous to one's health—even when not used as intended by the manufacturer.

CHAPTER 6

Space cadet

In the 1980s, the Department of Corrections did not treat mental health issues as they do now—the services were not readily available. Today (as a result of court cases) there are entire facilities that house and treat people with such issues within the department. This story is about my first interaction with an inmate in need of serious mental health services - I had no idea how to proceed.

Several weeks later, I was in my office dealing with another issue not covered in the employee orientation classes when I was interrupted by a knock on the door. I was relieved to see my mentor, Mr. Kirk, enter the office.

"Mr. Allen, will you be very long? We have an appointment to review the budget. Don't you recall?"

"Yes, I remember, but inmate Kent has a problem that perhaps you can help us with."

He glanced at his watch and said, "As long as it does not take much time. I have other appointments this morning."

I nodded gratefully and told Kent to start from the beginning as Mr. Kirk took a seat. Kent appeared to be a normal, rational human being; however, he had just informed me he was from outer space!

As stated by Kent, he hailed from the outer limits of a distant solar system. He was, in fact, part of a sleeper cell, a recently activated sleeper cell. He was to go to the prison yard at midnight in two days to receive instructions.

Kent suspected he would have little choice but to board the *mother ship* and be whisked light-years away, which presented two problems. The first problem was that he had zero interest in returning *home* or being a part of this cell. It would mean never seeing his family again, or at least those considered family. He did not want to exchange his current life for a life he did not remember. The second problem was that the prison yard closed at 9:00 p.m., and he was in his cell by 10:00 p.m. When he explained to the cell leader that he was in prison and the police would not let him out at that hour, the response was to *sneak out* as he did as a teenager, which was not as easy to do.

I glanced at Mr. Kirk, who nodded as if he understood completely, and it all made perfect sense. In mid-sentence, he cut Kent off with, "I think I got it," and offered a brief recap. Kent was from *outer space* and was ordered to complete his mission and return to his home planet. Kent, however, preferred to remain on planet Earth.

The inmate acknowledged this was the problem, and my friend and mentor, Mr. Kirk, claimed, "Not a problem. We can help you with this. We got this covered."

Kirk then leaned over to Kent and asked in a low voice, "So you're from outer space?"

Kent nodded.

Kirk glanced around, lowered his voice even more, and stated, "Guess what. So am I."

Oh, this is great, just great, I thought to myself, *I'm up in here with two nuts.*

But Kent's reaction was completely different. His entire expression changed. His face lit up, and he smiled for the first time that morning.

"Really?" Kent then asked the sixty-four thousand dollar question of which I was most curious. "Where are you from?"

Kirk dismissed his question with a wave of his hand and said, "So far away...not on these charts."

Kent understood because, as it turns out, his planet was far, far, away as well.

Suddenly Mr. Kirk switched gears and asked about the baseball cap Kent was wearing. Kent took off the hat and offered it to Mr. Kirk, who jumped. It was clear Kirk did not want to touch the cap; he directed Kent to place the cap on the desk.

After carefully examining the cap, Kirk asked if it was from the inmate canteen. The answer was yes; the inmate purchased the cap from the canteen.

Kirk pointed to a line of stitching and, in a low voice, said, "You see this? Well, don't tell anyone, but it is a signal blocker."

Mr. Kirk went on to say a community of *space aliens* was amongst the inmate population. (I wanted to state that he should include at least one staff member in this 'community' but remained silent.) Due to this *alien population*, the department started putting signal blockers in all the headgear sold in the canteen. When worn at the proper angle, the cap effectively blocks all out-of-space signals going to one's brain.

Kirk had inmate Kent to put the cap on his head and adjust it until the cap was at the proper signal blocking angle. Kirk suddenly switched topics again and asked if Kent had recently talked to the good people in the mental health department. Kent's answer was no. Mr. Kirk claimed a plan was underway to interview all inmates and suspected Kent would soon meet with the mental health staff. Like real soon. Like in a day or two.

During this meeting, Kirk urged Kent to tell them everything.

"Don't hold anything back because they know a lot about your situation anyway," said Mr. Kirk.

According to Kirk, the mental health staff monitors all radio signals coming into the institution. Kirk further suspected the medical team would most likely prescribe medication and extracted a promise from Kent to take the medications as directed. Since he started taking daily mental health medication, Kirk has not heard voices and no longer needs to wear a cap to block unwanted signals.

At that point, Kirk concluded the interview by thanking the inmate for his time. He told Kent that meeting and talking with him had been great, but he had urgent business to discuss with Mr. Allen. The entire interview took less than four minutes. As Kent returned to his duties, Kirk started to dial a telephone number. He paused to suggest I conduct a security check. I got his point. The entire conversation could have been a ruse to cover up nefarious activities.

When such an incident occurs, the noise level changes. First, it becomes quiet, or the noise level drops, then one hears the commotion from the incident, furniture moving, grunts, and so on. Next, all the inmates would be at the door attempting to exit. Because the noise level had remained constant, I did not expect to find anything amiss, and I did not.

As I left the office, I heard Mr. Kirk say to someone on the phone, "I got a live one for you. You need to put this one on the top of your list."

When I returned to the office, Mr. Kirk had concluded his call and was arranging budget spreadsheets on the desk.

He looked up and stated, "They - the mental health unit, are going to try to pull your boy in this afternoon for an evaluation. But they may not get to him until tomorrow. I told them it was urgent, and that homeboy was a danger to himself to others and a threat to the safety and security of the institution. Saying this always gets everyone's attention. I have seen them come as fast as an hour. But that was before we started receiving so many crazies. Now, can we please go over the budget?"

"First, I have a couple of questions. When you applied for this job, did you tell the State of California that you are from outerspace? Are you even a citizen?"

Mr. Kirk was silent for a moment. He then stated that a previous governor, who later went to a high position in Washington, D. C., had closed most mental hospitals years before. Before these closures, many of our current inmates would be in state mental institutions.

"I believe he has mental health concerns and should be elsewhere. We did not have much time, and I wanted to build up trust so he would take my recommendations seriously, and I believe he did. The proper people will review his case factors and determine his future housing and programming needs."

Mr. Kirk looked at his watch again. "This place is always full of crazies. Every time I come in here, all I see are lunatics. I'm beginning to think you attract them. Do you think you can keep the nuts out of your office for five minutes for us to review the budget?"

"I don't think so. At least not while you are in here."

"What, why not?"

"With you in here, there is still a nut left."

He smiled. "Make that two nuts!"

Postscript:

Mr. Kirk was my mentor and became a good friend. He was quick on his feet and imparted valuable information. A few days later, he took me to the medical department to introduce me to members of the mental health staff. He also provided a list of helpful in-service-training classes for me to take.

Offenders in serious need of mental health care are often at risk when housed with the general inmate population. Due to lack of treatment, their mental health does not improve. They are at risk of being victimized by smarter inmates and trade away valuables for less than they are worth. Some have been talked into engaging in criminal activity such as committing assaults. Due to reforms resulting in part from various lawsuits, mental health screening identifies inmates that require placement in treatment programs.

CHAPTER 7

Baby, where did our love go?

L *ooking for love in all the wrong places is a story as old as time. Like so many of us, some see what they want and ignore the things they choose to overlook or not notice. This story is about love found and later lost and takes place within 10 days. It is a story of a young inmate clerk leaving the workplace looking forward to a lifetime of bliss. And an employee -me - leaving the workplace looking forward to a few relaxing days off. Neither the inmate nor I could have guessed what the next several days would bring or that the next meeting would be our last.*

It was a Thursday afternoon, the start of a three-day weekend. Monday was a holiday, and Friday was my regular day off. I had a four-day weekend to look forward to, which I combined with comp time to add four additional days for a total of nine consecutive days off. *Comp time is compensation with time off instead of paid overtime.*

I was looking forward to enjoying some time away from work. The clock, however, was not cooperating. It was moving so slow it appeared to have stopped.

I had just rechecked my watch when inmate Decker approached and requested, "A word, a favor, really."

Decker was a pleasant guy, did his work, and had yet to cause any trouble, so I was not opposed to granting his request if possible.

In the past, inmates approached me regarding safety concerns and requested that I notify the appropriate personnel. He said he needed several minutes to provide the necessary background information. Not knowing if his problems were related to his safety, I told him to go ahead, and he described the situation.

Decker had been in prison before, about five years ago. While on the streets, life was uneventful, not living but more like existing. More often than not, he engaged in a daily struggle to survive. Illegal drug use helped him cope with life's complexities, which is why he returned to prison. He soon found life behind bars had changed very little. He slowly adjusted to the boredom of confinement without the use of drugs.

Then about three months ago, something happened. Decker met someone special, someone extraordinary, the love of his life.

"Okay, but what do you need from me?" I asked.

He asked for another minute or so, and he would explain. You see, he had found the person he had been searching for his entire life. And to think they met in prison, behind bars! He had never known love like this before and was unaware that emotions so intense were possible. All he knew was that he would never be lonely again. Even when apart, the two would be together in each other's hearts. And to think they were once strangers, but now soulmates. I thought he was being a tad optimistic and started to say so but decided not to.

Decker continued that most people go through life without finding their soulmate. There will never be another love for him. Bad times were in the past, with nothing but sunshine and blue skies ahead.

This time I did speak up and gently said, "Maybe you are reading too many books. Maybe switching to nonfiction or watching different television programs would help."

He smiled and made a slight motion with his head. He now had the feeling that only true love can bring. He was happy all the time, and the thing is, he never expected to find love behind bars. But one must grab onto love whenever it comes around. You must hold on with both hands and not let it get away.

By this time, I had heard enough and asked, "What exactly do you need from me?"

He asked for another minute or two of my time, and he would explain. You see, he had found the person he had been searching for his entire life. And to think they met in prison, behind bars. He had never known love like this before. He was not aware that such intense feelings were possible. He only knew that he would never be lonely again. Even when apart, the two would be together in each other's hearts. To think they were once strangers but now soulmates.

He was beginning to repeat himself!

Once again, I thought he was being a tad optimistic, but I have heard *love makes the world go round.* Decker continued to say that most people go through life without ever finding true love, and there will never be anyone else for him. His bad times were in the past. Nothing but sunshine and blue skies ahead. He never thought he would find the love of his life here, but one must grab onto love whenever it comes around. One must hold on with both hands and not let love slip away.

It was clear that he was having problems asking for the favor!

He was beginning to irritate me. I asked if he wanted something besides talk because I had a thing or two to do. Well, he did have a request, more of a favor, and if I could see fit to grant it, he would be very grateful. The soul mates lived in different housing units. Opportunities to be together were limited. Due to varying yard times and eating schedules, the two were often reduced to stolen glances across the crowded, noisy chow hall or 'accidentally' bumping each other in passing. It hurt to be away from the one you love. Love you can see, but not touch. It wasn't fair.

I interrupted and said, "Life often is not."

He continued to say that the few times the soulmates were able to spend time together, it was like magic or something. When the two were together, they both felt so alive. He shared things with his soulmate he had not shared with others, revealing parts of himself that no one else had ever seen. His future lover had done likewise. In past relationships, one person often loved more than the other. But the great thing was they cared for each other equally. Decker had finally found someone to call *his own.*

"The favor," I reminded him.

Well, the soulmates received permission to change cells and move in together. Today was that day. As we spoke, this new cellmate/soon-to-be lover was waiting for his arrival at their new abode. The two had big plans. They planned to stay in on the weekend and enjoy each other as never before. They had plenty of food, so there was no need for them to leave the love nest. They would watch television, listen to the radio, eat, and hang out.

The request: Could he go home early, as in right now, so they could start their life of bliss?

I reached for the Director's Rule Book and found Section 3045.2 Excused Time Off. As I suspected, consummating a relationship was not among the listed reasons for granting time off. I denied his request.

He smiled, thanked me for my time, and said, "Well, it was worth a try."

I suggested he return to his tasks with vigor, keep busy, and the time would pass quickly.

When the workday ended, he rushed to clean his area. He was the first inmate worker to leave. With a wave and slight grin, he bid me farewell. He practically floated out of the library and down the corridor to start his life with the one he loved. The next time I saw him, he was a completely different man.

That evening, while Decker and his soulmate were doing their consummation thing, I had left work and traveled north on Highway 101 to San Francisco. I was going to meet some old friends where good food would be eaten, and much laughter would occur. When I arrived, I wandered past the dancing into the kitchen. I found several people engaging in a spirited discussion. One gentleman, a professor of political science at a local community college, was relating a recent banking experience. He called it *banking while Black*. We were all African Americans.

The professor described how it started out as a typical day. Before class, he stopped by the bank to conduct business, as he has done numerous times. He did not notice anything amiss, but then his mind was elsewhere, and he was operating on autopilot. He was thinking about the midterm exam his class would be taking later that week.

Upon exiting the bank, the police greeted him. The professor stated the police threw him against the wall, placed him in hand restraints, and demanded the name and address of his *friend*. Perhaps the word *confronted* would be more accurate.

The perplexed professor asked, "Which friend?"

The police began yelling, screaming, and tightening the handcuffs. After a few minutes, the professor ascertained that a Black man had robbed the bank. The professor and robber had exchanged nods as the robber exited.

The professor explained to the police he was not acquainted with the robber and lacked knowledge of the robber's identity or his whereabouts. The professor further explained he was employed at the community college as an instructor and thus was not a bank robber.

The police removed the handcuffs to allow the professor to produce his college employment identification. The police also contacted the college to verify the information explaining that the professor was a *person of interest* in an alleged *bank robbery*. The college confirmed his employment. The police reluctantly released him and said he should remain available for additional questioning.

The professor stated it was fortunate he had completed his probation period, or his employment may have been in danger of termination. As it happens, his colleagues looked at him strangely for weeks, as if expecting the Federal Bureau of Investigation to storm the campus to arrest him. On the plus side, the dean of his department was an African American. He knew the police often erroneously detained and even shot men of color more often than others.

The conservative member of the group, an investment banker, noted the police have a necessary and challenging job and that all Black men are not innocent, to which we all agreed. He was the lone Republican in the group, but no one held that against him. Although he was a Republican, he was 'our' Republican. He wanted to know how the professor was dressed on the day of the incident.

The professor said he wore jeans, a starched shirt with a collar under a crew neck sweater, as most of his colleagues did. He was also wearing loafers without socks.

The investment banker said that was the problem in a nutshell. "Man, you are a college professor. Whenever you leave home, you should have on a three-piece suit with dress shoes highly shined."

The professor again pointed out his colleagues did not wear suits to work.

The investment banker countered with the rules for *brothers* were different. If the police see you walking down the street dressed in jeans, they will think you are just another unemployed brother. He further stated that when a Black professional is in his front yard raking the leaves, he should do so in a sports jacket with slacks. Someone asked if one should be wearing shined shoes as well.

After some thought, the investment banker replied that shined shoes were recommended but not required.

A couple of others related their stories of *living while Black*, but the professor's story was the most interesting until the investment banker shared his ongoing situation.

The investment banker and his wife purchased a house in a small beach town an hour or so north of San Francisco. The town had few residents of color. For the first six months, the police stopped him and his wife every day, twice a day or so it seemed. After being late for work a time or two, he began to leave 30 minutes early to allow for this police activity. He was detained, leaving and returning home. The police would check to ensure he had his driver's license and that his lights, brake lights, and signal lights were in working order; he had a relatively new car. Late one night, after midnight, the investment banker claimed he went into the kitchen and saw a patrol car parked across the street.

He further explained that all this activity resulted from the police department's deep concern for the well-being of him and his family. The police did not want anything untoward to happen to them. Or at least that was the way he chose to view it. According to him, to see it any other way would drive a brother crazy. Judging from the glances exchanged, most believed that the ship had already sailed. Someone urged him to continue to view the situation that way because *we don't want you going crazy.*

The conversation soon turned to politics as it often does. At the time, Reverend Jesse Jackson was making noises about seeking the Democratic presidential nomination. In discussing the pros and cons, none of us thought he had a reasonable chance of obtaining the nomination, although we were intrigued. According to the professor, Jackson had a decent opportunity to get a good number of delegates. However, most would likely fall short of the necessary number to win the nomination. Most of us agreed that an African American would occupy the White House one day. However, we all agreed it would not occur during our lifetime.

The professor made an interesting comment about the country's current political alignment. He said the first African American president would be from the Democratic Party and face unprecedented political and social opposition. If the man offers moral leadership -and it will be a man, not a woman - that portrays a sense of fairness speaking for those without a voice, as did other great presidents of this century, he will experience some success. One reason for this conviction was his belief that Black churches worldwide would keep the president and his family at the top of their prayer list. This would be partly due to concerns for the president and his family's safety.

Someone asked, "Surely you mean that all Christians would be praying for the first African American president?"

The professor replied while many Christians of all races would pray for the president, others would pray that harm befalls him and his family. The professor noted that many White Christian churches strongly supported slavery and the brutal treatment of enslaved people. Most southern White Christian churches failed to speak out against the violence experienced by people of color in their quest for equal protection guaranteed under federal law. By remaining silent while police officials and private citizens attacked and even killed Blacks attempting to vote, they condoned these violent terrorist acts. Not only were Blacks killed, but members of other races helping Blacks gain the right to vote became victims of assault, and some lost their lives as well.

The professor also said that one can find alliances between religious and political leaders from ancient times to the present. These were partnerships where the spiritual leaders were on the wrong side of history and morally wrong. Even the Nazis enjoyed some level of support from the church. As the son of a church deacon, he further explained that religious leaders turned Christ over to the Roman government officials demanding his execution.

In addition, conservative opposition to social progress was not limited to civil rights. It included each step of progress in the 20th century. Conservatives opposed the right of women to vote, women to join the workforce, labor unions, child labor laws, the eight-hour workday, the five-day work week, minimum wage laws, worker protection regulations, unemployment insurance program, the Social Security program, and medical care for the elderly.

The militant brother, an executive director of a community-based nonprofit organization in the East Bay, noted the professor might very well be correct. According to him, African American progress has always met with stiff resistance or backlash throughout American history. Whenever Blacks *stepped out of their place or reached above their station* and demanded rights the constitution claims all Americans are entitled to, violent resistance was often the result.

The landmark civil rights case Brown v. Board of Education mandated equal education for all students. Public schools were closed throughout the southern portion of the country, equally denying education for all students. Officials also created private academies for White students with vouchers bankrolled with public funds and/or tax-exempt status. At the same time, Black students found themselves without educational opportunities. Public schools in Prince Edward County, located in Virginia, were closed for five years. Over 100 congressmen from the south agreed to engage in massive resistance to this supreme court decision.

The militant said the civil rights gains resulting from the struggles we all witnessed growing up are being negated by the *war on drugs*, aka *war on Blacks*. This program was currently responsible for many young Black men in the criminal justice system. This includes over 25% of

Black men in some states, thus denying this group both current employment development and future voting rights. Our militant friend was the son of a Baptist preacher and a Sunday School teaching mother. When he came of age, he rejected the nonviolent philosophy of his parents. He adopted what he called the *Old Testament philosophy.* This was *an eye for an eye, a tooth for a tooth.* There was seldom any doubt which side of an argument he would take.

The discussion soon turned to reparations for slavery and comments made by an African American spokesperson employed by a conservative think tank. Based on our understanding, the gentleman's position was that the descendants of enslaved people should be the ones paying reparations when considering the standard of living enjoyed by Africans in America compared to Africans in Africa.

This concept was a bridge too far, even for the Republican in the group. He wondered out loud if the gentleman really believed this or was this a marketing ploy to obtain speaking engagements and future book contracts. "I guess 400 years of free labor was not payment enough for the brother."

The militant said marketing ploy or not, these comments gave aid and comfort to the enemy, aka racists. When pressed for an explanation, he said such statements provided cover to those downplaying the horrors of slavery, the damage suffered by enslaved families, the brutality of the institution itself, and the harsh 100 years of Jim Crow. He further said, after all, people will say they are better off here than in Africa.

According to our resident militant, the conservative mouth piece was a *house negro* and proud of that fact. He was the *worst kind of negro,* a dangerous negro, unlike someone harmless. He will make any statement or perform any act for a dollar, and because he has a PhD, people will listen to him. A man like that can put the entire race back to the Jim Crow era which had only ended 20 years ago. According to a college roommate, the militant was told that his direct, *in-your-face* manner made White folks uncomfortable; and that he could catch more flies with honey than vinegar. He is said to reply that Black folks became uncomfortable en route to the slave ship; besides, he had little use for flies.

While the group could not agree on whether the country should make reparations for enslaved families, everyone agreed the Negro's comments were so far *out of line they were off the chart*. The militant claimed many plantation owners received reparations for their loss of the enslaved after the Civil War. In contrast, the enslaved people themselves never received compensation for their role in the wealth creation of this nation. In addition, Blacks' historical, cultural, and other contributions to the American story are excluded from school curriculums and the public dialogue by design.

The professor noted the comments made by the spokesperson ignores the devastation, subjugation, theft of natural resources, kidnapping, and genocide done to Africa by various European powers. Thus, the living standards are higher in the recipient countries of the wealth stripped from Africa than those left impoverished. It also fails to take the Jim Crow period into account. The period that turned millions of Blacks into refugees escaping the horrors of the American south suggesting that the standard of living was not so great. For example, despite federal laws guaranteeing African Americans the right to vote, states' laws required the passing of various tests before voting. These 'tests' had questions like how many bubbles are in a bar of soap or how many seeds are in a watermelon? Per the professor, only God knows how many seeds are in an unopened watermelon, or (to paraphrase a television minister he watched, Pastor Foreman from San Jose), only God knows how many watermelons are in a single watermelon seed. They may as well have asked that question. The tests contained questions that no man could correctly answer.

After addressing other pressing world problems, we ran out of steam. Not long afterward, the party ended.

Before long, my vacation also ended, and I found myself walking up the corridor toward the central library. As I always did, I arrived at work 30 minutes early when I returned from several days off.

Decker was waiting at the East Gate and asked to speak with me. "It is very important," he said as we entered the library.

With a catch in his voice and the hint of a tear or two in his eyes, he told me a sad tale.

On the day we parted, Decker hurried to his cell where his new cellmate was waiting, and the two enjoyed their first time alone together. Because it was their new beginning, Decker wanted everything to be right. He had made purchases from the canteen of things his lover claimed to like. The couple spent an hour fixing dinner, the first of many shared meals to be. The following 24 hours were all Decker thought they would be, plus a whole lot more. Unfortunately, Decker soon discovered several unknown facts about his *soulmate*.

The *love of his life* was into one-sided sadomasochism. The *man he loved* enjoyed inflicting pain during what should be tender moments. The physical pain started on the third night, and the heartache moments later.

Sometimes the *loving* began with an assault, and other times it ended with an assault. Poor Decker never knew what to expect, aside from pain being a part of the experience. His *lover* believed it best to mix things up, making things more interesting. Decker thought that love should always feel good and never hurt. One should take the extra step to make the other person happy. He tried but was unable to *get with this pain thing.*

And there was one more problem. Decker was not only to satisfy his lover at night, but at other times he was to satisfy the desires of others for the price of a pack of cigarettes. The *soulmate* kept all the smokes because that is the way he rolls. He was in charge, or in his words, *he was the hog with the big nuts.*

After several days of this torture, Decker attempted to contact the sergeant who approved the cell move, but Sergeant Cole was on special assignment. Decker said he was too embarrassed to contact other staff members and waited for my return. Concluding his sad tale, he said, "I thought he loved me," and dropped his head on the desk and wept.

I quietly suggested he attempt to pull himself together while I make a telephone call. He nodded and began wiping his eyes.

When I finished my call, he wondered if his former lover would miss him or ever think of him. I gently noted some people only think of themselves. Decker nodded again and expressed hope his former lover would at least find his way out of that dark place. Paraphrasing the Good Book, I replied, some men prefer darkness to light. He nodded again.

A correctional officer arrived and escorted my clerk out of my office, the library, and my life.

Postscript:

In Ecclesiastes 1:9 Solomon wrote, "There is nothing new under the sun." Our surroundings may change, our situations may be altered, but the hearts of men remain deceptive. One can never be certain of another's motives. In Ecclesiastes 1:2 Solomon writes, "All is vanity." I believe Solomon is telling us, life is more than the sum of things happening *under the sun.* I believe the writer was talking about the emptiness of living only for today. We should never put all our hope, faith, and expectations of fulfillment in another person. Only God provides such fulfillment. People all too often show us parts of themselves they want us to see, causing disappointment and even hurt. Sometimes life can be painful and, at the same time, a learning experience. I hope that this was the case for inmate Decker.

CHAPTER 8

The marriage

*M*arriage is a legally recognized union of two people in a personal rela-tionship and establishes their rights and obligations. This story is about an inmate who learned a powerful but painful lesson about life and marriage. He found himself on the receiving end of the hurt he caused too many other people. The games he played in the past came back to him, much like a boomerang. This is ultimately about accepting responsibility and moving in a different direction.

Take the case of my first wife, a woman I met at a bus stop, she fell madly in love, but I did not. I mean, she was okay, but nothing to write home about. It was more of meeting my needs than anything else. I fell in love for the first time ever with *Baby Girl*, whom I met years later while serving time, as they say! This feeling was not puppy love stuff, but the real thing. I ought to know; I experienced that puppy stuff often enough. The fact that 90% of the things I told my first wife the day we met were lies; lies she should have recognized as a clue that I was not in love. Don't get me wrong; she was okay. I mean, she had a job, a car, and a decent place to stay, so what was there not to like? I told her what she wanted to hear the first day and most days that followed.

I continued this behavior up until the day I left. That morning as she left for work, I told her I had never loved anyone as I loved her, and no woman had ever made me feel like she made me feel. I also told her I would have dinner ready when she got home, and after eating, we would go to the movies, and after that, we would go dancing.

By the time she got home, I was long gone, of course. I took whatever cash she had on hand and a couple of things of value she would not miss right away. She wanted to hear lies, and I was happy to oblige. On the day we met, I told her I had a Bentley. I was on BART (Bay Area Rapid Transit) the public transport system, because my automobile was in the shop. Three months later, she still did not see or ride in my auto. Anyone else would have recognized the lie.

When we met, I was looking for a new place to stay. At the time, the woman I was with told me to get out and was constantly calling the police. I did not share this with my future wife; why should I? I just said my lease was up, and I might be leaving the area. Let's keep it 100% - who is honest these days. If more people were, there would be very few hookups.

When she told me she did not believe in living together without the benefit of marriage, I immediately proposed. I mean, this was the answer to my housing problem. I saw no point in telling her I was already in a relationship with two different women one of which was married. What good would that do? The entire time we were together, all I did was tell lies, some my wife caught, and others went right by her.

See, I never worked regular hours but had money most of the time. Most people would have asked questions, but not my wife. Okay, I have a weakness. I love the better things of life but hate to work. When I see something that I want, I take it, or one like it. Why work and save for it. That is so old school. By the time you save up money, the thing is obsolete. What good is that? And I cannot stand for people to tell me what to do, including her. I have no use for supervisors, except when in prison, where I obey most rules and regulations. I also follow my supervisors' instructions. The prison supervisors have badges and can make prison a living nightmare.

Another thing, I do not steal while incarcerated. Retribution is swift and can turn deadly. Once I saw an inmate place a package in a specific location. I went over and grabbed it. 'Finders keepers', right! Within minutes, I'm in the middle of several inmates holding shanks - knife-like objects, demanding the return of their property.

They explained that the rules of their gang required them to both retrieve their stolen property and stab the thief. They claim this served a dual purpose. It kept them from appearing weak and provided training opportunities in stabbing for new gang members and other members that had not stabbed anyone in a while. I was not to take the stabbing personally. It was just politics. The assault may not have been personal, but the infection certainly was. They could have at least used clean shanks.

This incident was a significant learning curve for me. I never saw things the same again. I now realize many people do not place the proper value on their lives, wellbeing, or even freedom. There are many crazy people in this world, none of which are wearing signs identifying them as insane. Say you bump into someone by accident, someone you do not know, especially in one of those states where everyone carries a gun. It is best to offer a sincere apology and move on. Not mad dog them - to stare a person down - like I used to do. You never know what someone else is going through. They may be planning to kill themselves that day and decide to kill you (for getting in their face) before killing themselves.

Some men decide to keep company with another man's wife or go into a store and pull a 211—penal code for armed robbery. That is plain crazy. I know people who lost their lives over stupid things like pulling a 211 with a fake gun. Such people do not value either their life or freedom. I was once like that, but not anymore. I also discovered that fast money never lasts long. It's like they say, *easy come easy go*.

Anyway, I first came to prison for the crime of spousal abuse when my girl (from a previous relationship several years back) and I parted. Or maybe I should say she moved out. We agreed I would place her things - most of the stuff in the apartment, to be honest - outside of our house. I complied with her request from the second story balcony. I tossed clothes, chairs, and tables, causing the furniture to break apart. When she saw the mess, she started screaming and hollering - that is when I grabbed the dishes.

Okay, I was a little drunk. Anyway, my girl tripped over some broken pieces of furniture. She banged her head and cut her arm, trying to run when I started throwing the dishes, cups, and glassware. Okay, so I was throwing knives when the police arrived. Only a few of the items hit her. The girl was not hurt. Everyone knows that wounds to the head usually bleed, and she only required a few stitches on her arm. I don't know why she took three weeks off work, other than laziness. The judge, district attorney, and public defender were all women. As soon as I saw them, I knew things would not go well and I would soon be en route to the *big house*.

The district attorney produced pictures of the driveway and played up the alleged victim's injuries. She claimed many of the items destroyed had belonged to the victim's grandmother. She called them antiques. As far as I could see, it was all worthless junk. It was so old it could not have been worth much. I mean, it was far from being new, so how much value could it have had?

The judge spent the entire trial glaring at me. My public defender did little defending, barely knew my name, and nothing about my case. Perry Mason, she was not. She claimed the character witnesses I provided lacked *character*. She claimed both were drunk when interviewed by her office. Of course, I was *found guilty*. I did not stand a chance in that kangaroo court.

The second time I came to prison, it was my public defender's fault again. My homeboy and I pulled this little job. During the trial, I testified that I was the victim of misidentification. I stated I was on vacation several hundreds of miles away when this crime occurred.

When asked to produce receipts as proof, I explained I paid cash and saw no need to keep receipts since I had no way of knowing I would be the victim of a false arrest. My girl - at the time - took the stand and backed me up. Course, I had to give her some dope for her trouble.

Well, as it turns out, the place had a working camera that filmed the entire incident. My crime partner told me it was fake. I now see why he took a plea deal. So, the district attorney had video footage of us robbing the joint. The district attorney threatened to file charges on my girl for lying while the judge used both hands to throw the book at me. That's when my girl started lying for real. She said she only lied because of fear I would harm her family if she failed to support my claims. So, I was soon back behind bars, locks, and gates.

Things seldom work out for me. I bounced around different institutions before settling in at Soledad State Prison. I eventually landed a job cleaning the visitor's room. The boss was okay, and I even received pay, eight cents per hour. Of course, I did not clear that much because I had to pay restitution.

So, one day, I am at work when these two fine women enter to visit an inmate. Well, only one was visiting the inmate. The other came along for the ride. I talked to the other one. Soon we were laughing and having a good time. Before leaving, she gave me her address, a post office box that should have raised the alarm, but I was smitten. I wrote her a letter that night; she responded. Soon we were exchanging several letters each month. After a while, she began to visit.

Her letters said she was from Persia and did not know many people in the States. However, she felt she knew a lot about American culture from movies, television shows, and other media outlets. She loved the fact that a woman could go where she wanted without a man's permission, and a person could go to the church of their choice, unlike in Persia.

I went to the library to locate information about Persia and its culture. The place is now called Iran, which was another clue I missed. Why didn't she just say she was from Iran? A person can never trust liars, and another thing, she never let me call. Of course, I would have to reverse the charges. I could not reimburse her because I only make eight cents an hour.

I had not enjoyed the company of a woman in a long time. I would stay up late writing her letters, pouring out my soul. I shared things and feelings I had never shared before and may never again.

I must admit I had always looked at what a girl could do for me. I agreed with the old school song *First I look at the Purse*. That was me! Whenever I met a woman, my first questions were, do you have a job, followed by what kind of car do you have? Of course, people lied a lot, so one must watch out for that. Some women claim to be employed, but you find out later they are on public assistance. Or they claim to own a condo, and it turns out they live in public housing. I tell you; people are just plain dishonest. Yeah, I played minor games with women, but I was for real this time. I cared deeply for this woman.

I still have her letters that I read from time to time. The letters talked about how she always wanted to come to the States and leave her life in Persia. She dreamed of enjoying the freedoms the States offered. In her home country, women had to dress a certain way and couldn't go anywhere without permission from a man. A woman alone was subject to being detained. The police would determine if she had permission from a man to be outside the home. I never told her this, but that sounded like a good system to me!

My favorite time of day became when staff passed out mail. Whenever I received a letter from her, it became - what my granny called - a *red-letter day*. That is to say, a memorable day. I found myself developing unfamiliar feelings for this woman, something I was unaware I was capable of having.

Longing for her next visit, I often re-read all her old letters. Weeks turned into months, and soon, I realized we had been together for an entire year. Around this time, the subject of marriage came up. She had applied for American citizenship and wondered out loud if being married would enhance the application. I assured her it would and suggested we get married without delay. After several weeks of discussions, she agreed.

I had to jump through several hoops before we could get married. For example, I had to obtain fake divorce papers because my file indicated I was married. A guy from G–Block hooked me up to get this done. It just shows how little the staff knew. I had several wives and had yet to get a divorce. I was grateful that places produced fake driver's licenses, passports, and of course, divorce papers.

I explained to her we could have a conjugal visit after marriage. It would not be for six months, but it was an event we should start planning along with the wedding.

We were married in a simple ceremony and spent the rest of the day sitting on hard plastic chairs, holding hands, drinking cokes, and eating vending machine food. I had never seen a more beautiful bride, and I found the entire scene strangely romantic; hard chairs, lousy food, and all. She thought of everything, including extra money for the vending machines and a wedding gift. She brought me a ring. She arranged to place the jewelry on my inmate property list. This day was the equivalent of a month of *red-letter* days.

She completed her part of the matrimonial visit application. Five months later, we received a date for our three-day visit. The night before the great consummation, I was awake all night. I was far too excited to sleep. I began preparing for the big day weeks before. My hair was tight. My clothes were clean, pressed, and starched. My shoes were shined to a high gloss. I believe a person should always make an effort to look their best. Some inmates appear to get their clothes from the housing unit dumpster, but not me, and I put an extra effort into my appearance that day.

I was the first inmate to arrive at the family visiting office. Since it had yet to open, I found myself pacing in front of the door. Eventually staff and six other inmates arrived. After 10 minutes, officers and a sergeant opened the outer office doors. I noted with a great degree of pride that I was the sharpest guy there. A couple of guys looked like they had put on clothing straight from trash bins without even washing and ironing.

We took seats, and the officer called us in one at a time. Eventually, I was the only inmate in the outer office, and I could hear loud laughter from the other room. I wished they would dispense with the jokes and get with the program. Then, finally, it was my turn.

The middle-aged sergeant called me son and said, "Son, your visitor has yet to arrive."

"What, what did you say?" I shouted.

"I said your wife is not here. She is a no-show. She has not come. As far as I can determine, she has not called the institution. You can use my phone to make a call if you wish. I have been trying to reach her without success. Do you have a number for her?"

The sergeant was being kind. He explained the phone number was valid when the application was approved, showing me the employee's section noting the interview with my wife. However, it did not appear to be a working phone number now. I did not have another phone number for her and so informed him.

He suggested I call on the outside chance he had misdialed. I called the number on the visiting application, only to find the number was no longer in service. The two officers started snickering. The sergeant glanced in their direction, and they stopped.

The sergeant said he left a message with the switchboard to call him if my visitor called or arrived. After a few seconds delay, he declared they had to go as they had other duties requiring their attention elsewhere. He asked if I would be in my cell, at work, or on the yard and where he could reach me quickly if she arrived. The sergeant was being kind because he said if she came before 1:30 p.m., he would allow my visit. He finished work at 2:00 p.m., so 1:30 p.m. was the best he could do. Generally, if a visitor did not arrive at the appointed time, they had to reschedule. But he could tell I put in a lot of effort. There were more snickers.

I know he meant my clothes were together. My jeans contained so much starch they stood up by themselves. See, it pays to look your best. I couldn't go to work; everyone knew about my visit. I could not go to the yard; I would get dirt on my clean clothes. I did not want to sit in my cell staring at the four walls but concluded that was the best option. I did not want to be around people.

I paced the cell in a broody mood. Suddenly, I felt the need to get off my feet. My legs were not very steady, and I did not trust the starch in my jeans to hold me up. Visions of her laid out on the side of the highway kept running through my mind. This day had to be one of the worst days of my entire life. I began the day with high hopes and expectations, only to have events come crashing down all around me.

I did not eat lunch, go to dinner, or go to the night yard. I also could not watch television or listen to the radio. I just sat in my cell staring at the concrete walls. I fell asleep and dreamed about my girl and me in the visiting trailer during the night.

Then I woke up. The dream had been so authentic it was cruel, for when I woke, I was in my cell alone. At least I did not have to deal with my cellmate, who was pending release from the Administrative Segregation Unit and not due back for a couple of days. It occurred to me if I stayed in the cell, no one would know that I didn't go to the visiting trailer. So, I decided to remain in my cell. I was not in the mood to deal with people anyway.

The next day I sort of heard from her. My letter to her was returned stamped *Return to Sender moved no forwarding address.* At least that is what I remember it said. I ripped up the letter and tossed it. It was one I posted about two weeks ago. As best as I could recall at the time, I had sent six letters in the past two weeks. As it happens, the correct number was eight. Now mail time became the worst time of day. The day after I received the sixth returned letter, I woke up smelling the coffee. My girl had played me; the whole marriage/relationship thing was a setup. She married me to enhance her citizenship application. She was now (or close to being) a US citizen, thanks partly to my foolishness.

When she was a no-show for the significant visit, I thought I was at my lowest point. I was wrong. That point was still around the corner and up the street. When I needed her to come around, write, or even call the institution to let me know she was alright. She did neither! I tell you; the whole thing was a setup. But one day, she will pay. She will meet someone who will do her wrong. *Baby* will never come across another guy like me, a man who will love her and treat her right.

I got a pass to the inmate law library and explained my situation to the inmate law clerk. He said his name was Shaw, but everyone called him *Lawyer*. I told him the whole story and said I wanted this marriage annulled immediately and her arrested for fraud. I was ready to press charges.

The clerk told me to have a seat, and he would be with me in a bit. When he came to my table, he asked if I wanted some java and returned with two cups of coffee. After taking a seat, and a sip of coffee, he explained that an annulment might not be the best way to proceed because we were never legally married. He further stated I ran the risk of catching another case by pursuing this matter.

According to the clerk, they put people in prison for getting remarried before getting a divorce. Who would have guessed that? I mean, I knew it was against some rule or regulation, but prison? I thought maybe a two-dollar fine or something. So, there was nothing I could do to thaw her game. I left the library and returned to my cell.

I wondered if *Baby* had found out about my previous marriages. Shaw thought this was a possibility. Maybe she did find out I was indeed a *bigamist* and thought I was the one running a game. When I reflected on my various games, cons, misdeeds, and scams, I came to myself. The thought of my past behavior being the source of my current discomfort was more than I could stand. I had to move on. I had no choice. The fact that I may have chased my love away by my past actions was something I could not dwell on, a place I did not want to go.

As I sat in my cell, I thought back on some of the other games I played. Games like packing my bags, walking toward the door while the woman stood by crying, begging me to stay. I would reach the door and announce this was so long, goodbye and farewell. I must admit it did not work one time. The woman said *okay*, sat on the couch, and watched me leave. It was raining that night and very cold. After a couple of blocks, I returned to the apartment and was in the process of telling her that I was willing to give her a second chance when I noticed the gun in her hand. I stopped talking. She asked, "Do I look like I want a second chance?" She raised the gun level to my mid-section and said, " You best step your sorry behind away from my door before I fill it with lead."

I started stepping and did not stop until I reached a flophouse halfway across town that rented rooms by the hour. I booked a room for fourteen hours, enough time for me to rest and plot my next move. I was so tried, that I feel asleep within minutes of entering the room. I woke up an hour or two later and realized that I was not alone. There were bugs in the bed, rodents running on the floor and insects everywhere else. When I called the clerk to complain, she laughed and said 'a room by yourself cost more' and hung up. This caused me to refine my act.

I would tell the woman that if I leave, she would never see me again once I walked out of the door. If she appeared indifferent to the thought of me leaving I would change the subject. However, if she began to cry, begging and pleading for me to stay I would continue the charade. I would begin extracting concessions. I would make her agree to certain changes. As I reached the door sometimes with my hand on the door-knob - it was an act I developed - I would agree to remain if she promised to do this or that. The truth was I had no place to go and had no intentions of leaving. I would leave if I had somewhere to go when she was not home. The woman would return to an empty apartment. Sometimes I would leave a note, sometimes not. I never claimed to be an angel. I reflected on the pain I caused so many women, sometimes just for the heck of it or maybe because I could. It may have been a power trip on my part. It was hard to say why I did the things I did.

A few days later, I ran into Shaw, aka *Lawyer*, in the dining hall. He told me to come to the library when I got a chance as he wanted to run a few things past me. He was busy when I arrived, so he waved me to a seat and said he would join me *in a second*. Again, he came to the table with coffee and stated that he wanted to share a few things.

He wanted to know if I had thought about what we discussed in our last conversation and that he had a couple more things for me to consider. He restated his opinion that I should not assume *Baby* had *run a game* since there were other reasonable options to consider. *Baby* may have discovered my marital history on her own or been informed by the Immigration and Naturalization Service.

The *Lawyer* said that each county in the state has an Office of Public Records where a person could look up marriages and divorces. You said she was a beautiful woman...maybe some jealous guy went to the county office, searched the records, and suspected you were a bigamist. Or perhaps it was a concerned friend, or maybe she went herself.

His whole point was that my hands were not clean. I would have had a more precise idea of what was happening had I been honest about my past relationships.

He followed his first point with something else I had not considered. According to Shaw, people have engaged in fake marriages to enter the country and stay, and some try to become citizens. Perhaps the government had investigated her application and concluded the union was a fraud based on my marriage history. If so, she may have been arrested. This information was hard to take, a bitter pill to swallow. So, according to Shaw, there were several possibilities. None were good, but one worse than others.

When I returned to my cell, I pondered the issues Shaw raised. Maybe Baby did find out about my previous marriages. I did tell her I had never been married. In a way, this was true. I never considered myself married; my wives were married, not me. She may have thought I was running a game, but I was not; my feelings and most of my conversations were genuine.

Again, the thought that my past behavior may be responsible for my current anguish was difficult to take. The knowledge that my past may have chased the love of my life away from me was also more than I could stand.

Once again I thought back on the pain I caused with the games I played. Games like packing my bags, walking toward the door while the woman stood by crying, begging, and pleading with me to stay. Once a woman cried so hard that she began to hyper-ventilate.

The following week, I returned to the library bearing *a shot of coffee* for Shaw, planning to look at a few magazines or a newspaper or two. Shaw said he wanted to talk and produced some hot water for the coffee. He even had some sugar and cream. Shaw stated he wanted to share some thoughts on life from an older man to a younger man about various laws.

I interrupted and stated he had already told me about the state, federal, and local laws. He said he was referring to different laws.

Legal laws govern society while other laws, such as gravity govern nature. Few would argue that gravity or the legal system exist. However, many are unaware that spiritual laws also exist, which he wanted to talk about today.

According to Shaw, several great world religions include the *golden rule concept*. Another theme he shared is the concept of *reaping and sowing,* or *what goes around comes around.* If a person plants cotton, he reaps cotton, sows corn, he reaps corn. Basically, what a farmer plants, he later gathers from his fields. And according to Shaw, one always reaps more than he sows. One can plant a single apple seed and reap a tree of apples.

He said that, "as a man more advanced in years than yourself, I want you to know the same is true in life. What one sows is what that person reaps. If a person does not like what he is reaping, I always suggest checking out what they are sowing".

I must have looked doubtful because he said I had already proven this concept. He had provided coffee the other day, and today I arrived with coffee. If he had not given me coffee, it is doubtful I would have come with coffee.

Shaw smiled and said, "What one sows, one reaps. In this case, I sowed and reaped coffee."

He stopped smiling and said how we treat others often results in the way others treat us. In other words, things we do to others; others later do to us. Reconsider your relationships with women. As long as one is looking for gain, a positive experience is not likely to occur. Instead of looking for money, or a free place to stay, seek things the two of you can share and enjoy together.

"So, if I go around treating everyone nice, everyone will be nice to me, right? Is that the way it works?"

"No, jerks are all over." Shaw looked around. "There are even jerks in this room." We laughed. "However, if we constantly engage in evil acts, we can expect evil to pursue us, surround us and eventually overtake us."

Shaw then shared a story about an old man who lived on a country road en route to a large town. One day as he sat on his porch, a man asked for a drink of water. He also asked about the distance to the next town and the people who lived there. The old man on the porch asked where he was from and about the people who lived there. The traveler replied he was from a small town 10 miles up the road, and the people were great. The town was full of kind, generous, good-hearted people. He hated to leave, but his job transferred him.

The guy on the porch stated, "Well, I expect that you will find the same kind of people there."

An hour or so later, another man from the same area stopped for water. It must have been a hot day. He also wanted to know what kind of people he could expect to encounter in this particular city. In response to the old man's question, the man stated the people in the town he had just left were mean-hearted, cruel, and unwilling to offer a helping hand to others. The guy on the porch stated the traveler would find similar people in the city to which he was traveling.

But Shaw had more on his mind. He wanted to talk about one other subject. That subject was forgiveness. In Shaw's opinion, I needed to forgive my girl for committing fraud if, in fact, she did. Shaw said that if she was the type of person to take advantage of, and use others, then hating her was only hurting me. He pointed out I did not give much thought to the females I had wronged in the past, and neither would she if she was that type of person. I needed to get on with my life, to develop and grow as a person. He urged me to live in the present, look to the future, and forget the past.

Shaw glanced around the room and continued, "not every man in here has enjoyed the company of a beautiful woman, and you had that privilege while in prison. That is incredible. Savor the moments of laughter and the good times you shared. Those special moments belong to just the two of you. You may not have a future to share, but the two of you will always have that past. She was good for you and drew out a part of you that you were unaware existed. You can have that again. Don't go back; go forward."

If my former fiancé returned to Iran due to my dishonesty, I also needed to forgive myself. I need to live in the present and be careful of what I sow because it affects my future.

I was not sure Shaw knew what he was talking about but listening to him was better than listening to the thoughts running around in my head. I sat in the library until closing and returned the following day after work. I soon found myself in the inmate library several times a week.

I needed a change. I had enough negativity to last for years and hanging out at the library was a good start. I talked to the librarian about a job, and several months later, he hired me. That is how I came to be a library worker. The assignment is not perfect, but it has its moments. For example, a few months ago, a guy came in wanting information about appealing his case. He explained his sentence was 1,000 years to life. That meant he had to serve 1,000 years before parole consideration. I found out later he was only doing 325 years. He only told people he was doing 1,000 years so they would think he was crazy and stay away from him. Anyway, I thought about his situation and thanked God for not having a sentence of 325 years, which was the same as 1,000 years for all practical purposes.

It is easier to find things to be grateful for these days. Well, a few days ago, the inmate returned to the law library all excited; he had gotten action on his appeal. The court reduced his sentence from 325 years to 100 years. I found it difficult to share his excitement until he explained that people live to be 100 all the time. "I see them on that morning television show, but nobody lives to be 300. Besides, I am raising other issues the court has yet to rule on." He passed out cigars, and we celebrated with him, wishing him luck.

While busy, I did not think of her. Things began to change for me by being active, and this is how I learned to cope. So, when I started at the library, I would complete my chores and look around for more ways to help. I was tired of pushing a broom, and I had lost interest in running scams. That is how I discovered the law books. The law clerks would be overwhelmed with requests, so I would step up to help. I learned the locations of the various codes. At some point, I started reading law books to pass the time. I began thinking about my case considering what I had learned. I began to suspect my current prison sentence was incorrect, and I had received more time than my case factors required. I voiced these concerns to Shaw, who offered to investigate it for me.

A few weeks later, Shaw said I was right and that my sentence was incorrect, and would I like to appeal? I was speechless. By my calculations, each of my past prison sentences had been miscalculated and not in my favor!

Shaw asked again, "Would you like to appeal?"

"What?" I almost shouted. "Do I want to appeal? Does a hog want slop? Yes, I want to appeal like right now."

Shaw gave me a list of books to review. Each night I stayed up late reading. Together we worked on the appeal until Shaw was satisfied. It was filed and eventually granted.

My successful writ reduced my time to serve by several years. I said the job had its moments—well, that was one of them. A huge moment! I now only had about two years left to serve. I love working with law books and found I had a talent for it. I spent several hours each day during something I enjoyed, something positive. Sometimes helping someone file appeals, sometimes suggesting they try to settle in and do their time.

Since I gained a positive outlook on life, I am better. I get to fight injustice in and out of the prison by appealing sentences and prison disciplinary reports. It feels good to make a positive difference in someone's life. I got out of the fast lane. I plan to become a paralegal when I get out.

A seismic shift can force a person to change directions. Sometimes one has to hit rock bottom before finding one's purpose in life. That is what this whole *Baby thing* did for me.

I started reading books on philosophy and religion. I came across a book in the Old Testament, Book *of Proverbs*. I stumbled upon passages that spoke to my condition:

Proverbs 11:18, *A wicked person earns deceptive wages,*

and

Proverbs 22:8, *Whoever sows injustice will reap calamity.*

This sounded like the story of my life. The calamity part anyway. The concept that one suffers or benefits from their actions was new to me or not something I had previously considered, at least not in this way. Bad things follow bad people, and negativity has certainly followed me.

After giving the matter a great deal of thought, I concluded *fast money* does not last and seldom is worth the effort. Say a person pulls off a series of robberies and nets 50,000 dollars before getting caught and going to prison for five years. That is only 10,000 dollars a year. People could net more working at a fast-food joint and keep their freedom.

Instead of working for minimum wages, I am in prison, earning 10 cents per hour. Yet as I look around at my fellow inmates, many are unemployed, while others have job assignments without pay. With the mandatory deductions from my income, it takes me a week to make enough to buy a decent bar of soap.

But I have an income and an assignment I enjoy. This fact alone makes me better off than many others - something I had not realized before. When I parole this time, things will be different. Life will still be a challenge, but life is always challenging.

POSTSCRIPT:

Proverbs 11:18 says, "A wicked person earns deceptive wages, but to him, that soweth righteousness shall be a sure reward." There is a contrast between those who pursue evil and those who pursue good. Those who sow deceitfulness will reap deceit. There is no escaping this judgement. If one has life, one can change their direction, stop chasing evil, and pursue good.

CHAPTER 9

Born under a bad sign

In this story, the main character understands why things seldom work out for him and believes that fate dictated events before he was born. This is about a man who fails to take responsibility for his actions and sees no need to change his behavior. The problem lies elsewhere, and others need to change.

See, it's like this. *Baby* and I were in this store when she started talking aloud and acting a fool. Against my better judgment, I put her in check while in the breakfast cereal aisle. I checked her from time to time, but only when she got out of line! Usually, I wait until we are alone, but I decided not to this time. In my experience, all women require checking from time to time, some more than others.

Baby would get out of line every couple of months, thus slapping her around would put things back in order. All the men I know agreed. Checking is something a woman has got to have. They need it. A couple of women even told me that keeping them in check proved I loved them. I agreed. If I did not genuinely care for them, I would not make an effort to correct them.

On this particular day, *Baby* just wanted attention. I had put a box of corn flakes in the cart when she started hollering and screaming that she was sick of cornflakes and wanted Rice Krispies. Well, I was tired of cold cereal, period, and was being nice by accepting only two hot meals a day: lunch and dinner. If she would cook breakfast, we would not be having this conversation.

I should have left the store but remained and continued to talk. I started checking - with my fists - when she said she was not a maid or a cook. I had heard this song before and was in no mood to listen to it again.

Baby told me she needed to be kept *on a tight leash* on day one. She was not lying! Unfortunately, a woman I know landed in the hospital due to checking. I guess her man got carried away. I never believed in all of that. It is never okay to cause permanent injury. It can bring problems with the law; plus, it may hinder her in performing her duties. I told *Baby* on day two I did not care if she was on crutches; I expected my food to be ready on time. Some women balk at first but tend to get with the program after being checked a couple of times.

Sometimes I do a *pre-check*. One day I overheard a telephone conversation she was having. She did not realize I was in the room. She thought I went to the bathroom, but I eased back to the door to hear what she and her girlfriend found so fascinating. It turns out she was asking about some man she met at a club. I entered the room, snatched the phone from her hand, and went upside her head several times. That was a pre-check. She had not done anything wrong yet but was thinking about it.

As mentioned earlier, I usually would wait until we were home or alone before checking her. But see, this time was a little different. On the way to the store, she complained that I did not have a job. Then in the store, she went off about the cereal. A man can only take so much!

I don't do the *regular job* thing because I am not a regular guy. I don't like following orders; I want to call the shots. That is the way I roll. Besides, even if I looked for a *regular job*, it would just be a waste of time. Unemployment is always high in my community. If not for the drug trade, a brother would starve to death.

The other day I saw this Black guy on television say that slavery was the only time there was full employment in the Black community. During slavery, every Black person in America had a job, teenagers, adults, everybody was employed. Even Black children barely able to walk were working. Working conditions were harsh, pay nonexistent, but hey, all Blacks had jobs. This is proof that having a job is overrated.

See, she wanted me to check her, and I obliged. I was just getting started when someone tapped me on the shoulder and said, "That is not the way to treat a lady."

People should stay out of other people's business. What happens between a man and his woman is between the two of them. So, I turned and saw a guy so old, he had grey hair.

So, I asked, "You want some of this?"

He shrugged and said, "I see you can hold your own against a woman, but how do you do against a man?"

I did not want to hurt the old man, so I said, "Look, grandpa, if you don't get up out of my business, I am gonna knock those false teeth out of your mouth."

But instead of leaving, he said, "I see that you can wail away on a 100–pound woman, but how good are you against a 165-pound man?"

"She weighs 125 pounds, and I am gonna teach you to stay out of grown folks' business," I said.

He said something about being a policeman, and I asked about his badge, "I don't need no stinking badge," he said.

Yea, that old movie line. So, I told him he would wish he had two or three badges when I got through with him.

Well, this entire encounter was more than I could stand. I was already having a bad day. So, I stepped over to the senior citizen pushing my girl aside. I realized I pushed harder than intended when she fell to the floor, banging her head on a shelf on her way down.

I remember saying to the old man, "This will not take long."

The next thing I remember is looking up at a guy asking if I was okay. I mumbled something and tried to get up, but nothing seemed to be working.

The guy said, "Don't try to get up. You may be hurt, don't worry, the police are on the way."

"What, the police?" I started struggling harder to get up and put some distance between me and that place. The last thing I wanted to do was talk to the police.

But it was too late. The police arrived. One stood watching me while the other one went to talk to the old grey haired guy. The two appeared to know each other. They were acting like friends.

The other officer came over to me and informed me I was under arrest for attempted assault on a police officer. Of course, they ran my record and found I had a couple minor warrants for jaywalking, failure to appear in court, and spousal abuse, all petty stuff.

So, I get hauled off to jail for attempted assault on a peace officer, checking my girl, making false statements, and other crap. How is checking my girl even a crime? It shows what kind of world we live in. A man cannot even check his woman. Plus, I get booked for the warrants. I had to stay in jail pending court proceedings based on the district attorney's false claim. He claimed I was not trustworthy because I failed to appear in previous cases.

But my attorney, the public defender, had good news days later. The elderly guy was not just off duty; he was on *administrative leave* because he had shot some child. My attorney thought we had a good chance of reducing the charges, if not beating the case outright if we could prove the guy was unstable. Plus, my attorney said that the shooting was all over the media. Experience taught me not to put much stock in public defenders. Whenever a public defender represents me, I always get mentally ready for prison. So far, I have ended up in custody each time. Still, I was cautiously optimistic. I mean, with a cop under suspicion, maybe I would get justice for once.

It turns out I was right to be wary. The media covered the story since the cop was already in the news cycle, and under suspicion. This story received extensive coverage in the local press with a twist casting my alleged police victim as a hero. He saved a woman from a vicious beating by a crazed criminal. The media played up my arrest history. They did not bother to distinguish between arrests and convictions.

Some press stories suggested a connection between the child shot by the police and me. According to media reports, the child shot by the police was my brother, cousin, neighbor, or family friend. These were all lies, and I could prove it. Just ask anyone who knows me. They will tell you I never watch the news, nor read the newspapers. I do not see the point. If one compares yesterday's headlines to a newspaper from 10 years ago, they would be the same: war, crime, floods, earthquakes, tornadoes, and fires. Same crap, just a different day, different year, or decade. So, I had never heard of the policeman, the child he shot, or any controversy surrounding the case. These were all lies to sell newspapers. They were all making money while I sat in jail. An innocent man. One minute I was with my *Baby* minding my own business, the next sitting in a cell awaiting trial without bail. Life is not fair. Not even close.

Next, the public defender comes with an offer from the district attorney of 15 years for a guilty plea to a host of charges. Now, this guy was making headlines at my expense right before the election. If I refused, he said he would go for a life sentence under the three-strikes law or the habitual criminal statute. According to the district attorney, I qualified for both. We eventually settled on a term of 10 years, which means I could be out in five years with a lot of luck, something that has always been in short supply.

I must admit I bear some responsibility for my current situation. I should have waited until we were home before putting *Baby* in check. If I had done so, I would not be in prison today; at least on this beef. An example of how unfair life is, *Baby* is not allowed to visit. According to the jail officials, she is one of my victims.

While in the county jail, I called her - reversing the charges - and suggested we get married when I get to prison which would allow us to have conjugal visits. She agreed. Well, the state now had the same rules as the county. My counselor told me she was my *victim*; thus, no visits of any kind, not even to get married. My girl said we could still get married and said something about having a proxy wedding. I said, "Great, and then you and the proxy go on a 'proxy'honeymoon. Forget the wedding. Start sending me packages and put some money on my books," and I hung up.

Then a strange thing happened. I stopped hearing from my girl. She stopped accepting my phone calls. The only package I received was a big envelope with my unopened letters proving she had received them.

It took me a minute to process all of this. You see, the prison is called Soledad, but I call it Sillydad because they have a bunch of silly rules with a bunch of stupid employees. It must be a job requirement; you got to be a fool to get hired at this place. It is probably on the application,'ONLY FOOLS NEED APPLY.' Sometimes I think I am the only one in the world with sense.

In any event, I found out there was a problem when I went to the canteen. I had already told *Baby* to rush money to my books the day we talked about the wedding because I had turned in my canteen order. That was one of the silly rules. An inmate cannot walk up to the canteen like a grocery store. You must turn in your canteen order days in advance. Another thing, it is not easy to get to the phone. During this crisis, I asked a correctional officer to let me out of the cell to use the phone. He looked at me like I was crazy, said no, and kept walking. I know it was not my phone time, but he could have made an exception, another one of those silly rules.

So, I get to the canteen thinking everything is everything. That is to say, everything was okay. I would have my order, go back to the cell, and chill. When I got to the window, the clerk pointed to the *bad news list* as people behind me started laughing. The list labeled *bad news* provides the names of inmates with insufficient funds to purchase canteen items. It was right there on *front street*. Everybody could see I lacked funds. I had not bothered to check the list as *Baby* had always done as I told her.

That was when I knew something was up. A few days later, I was allowed a phone call. When the operator asked, "Will you accept a collect call from a prison inmate?" I heard a click. I broke down and called her mama. When the operator asked the same question, her mother said, "No, and tell that fool to quit calling here."

Then, as Marvin Gaye would say, I figured out what was 'going on'. That woman was listening to her mama who never liked me. Even though I was the best thing that ever happened to *Baby*, her mama always bad-mouthed me. I explained to Baby her mama was jealous 'cause' we had a good thing going. Her mama just wished she had a good man like me, her being single and all. She was alone. I told *Baby* that she, *Baby*, would be by herself if she kept listening to her mama. I later got a letter from my sister saying that *Baby* was seen around the hood with someone else, some dude with a steady job. How low can a person go?

Some people will fall for anything! She settled for some ordinary guy with a nine to five job. I bet he even got taxes taken out of his check. If she wanted to lower her standards, that's on her. I have never held a nine to five job in my life except in prison. While on the streets, I operate by the seat of my pants. I brought excitement into her life. During our special moments, she would say things like, *No one has ever made me feel the way you make me feel. I have never loved anyone as much as I love you.*

I know, *Baby*, this relationship will not last. All I have to do is wait. It has been a year since I last heard from her. I expect a letter any day now. Every day it does not come means I am closer to hearing from her. I saw that on a television talk show about *breakthroughs.*

So, I get to Soledad State Prison. The *Soledad brothers* made the prison famous in the seventies or the sixties. After nine or 10 months, I got assigned to the inmate law library. This assignment—or any full-time assignment—adjusted my release day. Now I was looking at a release date in four years instead of eight. Unfortunately, that job only lasted a few months. But that was not my fault. I was unaware of the librarian's policy of having all inmate workers' cells searched when law books are missing. I would not have stashed the *missing books* in my cell if I had known.

The cops found the missing books in my cell, but that was not my fault either. It was the fault of my clients. We were to meet in the chapel to exchange books for cigarettes. The deal was for half down, and the balance was due upon delivery of the books.

The day after I got busted and fired, those fools came looking for their *merchandise*. I bitterly explained I no longer possessed their *merchandise*, seeing how the cops confiscated everything. The books were back in the library beyond my reach since I no longer worked there.

Those fools then said they wanted their *merchandise* or the return of their cigarettes. I told them I did not have either. See, I placed a bet on the Lakers, unaware of a couple of injuries among the starting lineup. None of this was my fault. So, they told me that was my problem and that I had 24 hours to produce either one. I told them to find some rocks to kick and get away from me.

I understood they were under pressure. But I could not go around making other people's problems mine. They started a jailhouse law firm with offices on the central yard. They were open seven days a week, 10 hours per day, and business was booming. They conducted interviews on the yard while the research and typing would occur in their cells. The stolen books were critical to their business model because the library was not open every day.

When the library was open, one needed a pass to navigate the corridor to the library's location. Operating out of the library - like their competitors, limited the amount of work they could take. They also needed a steady supply of legal materials, and I was their inside guy. The best part of the deal was their clients paid in cash. Family members sent checks to the *law firm* before the firm did any actual work. I was to get a cut. It was to be a long–term relationship. They claimed a late release from the cellblock prevented them from reaching the chapel. Well, that was not my fault. I made it to the chapel. I did my part.

I never liked the librarian. He was a big-time loser. I mean, one day, an inmate worker was a few days from parole. When he went to the supervisor to sign out, Mr. Allen asked about his plans. The inmate lied. He told Mr. Allen he had a job lined up with a landscaping company. Mr. Allen said that was great. He advised him to stay away from drugs, criminal activity and not waste his money on fast living. The inmate returned from the office and told us what Mr. Allen had said. We all laughed; what a loser.

The paroling inmate did not have a job lined up as a landscaper. He planned to return to his former occupation of selling pleasure products, aka illegal drugs. As for *fast living*, what is the point of having money, or even being alive, if not for fast living? That is the whole point of life. I must admit I was surprised to see the inmate back in prison less than a year later with a life sentence. This three-strike thing is killing people. However, Mr. Allen did not seem surprised. When the inmate saw the librarian, all Mr. Allen said was, *I guess that landscaping job didn't work out.* One day the librarian did not show up for work. The next day he told someone that he had been drunk. We all thought, *wow, maybe he has a life after all.* It turns out he was joking. His grandmother had a medical appointment or something.

And he was always saying dumb stuff. One day, I complained that I was always missing my breaks because an inmate decided he needed a law book. According to the librarian, my job was to serve the customers. I said these were inmates, not customers. Mr. Allen pointed toward the door and said that out there, they are inmates; when they enter the library, they become customers. I explained to the librarian this particular customer - the source of this complaint - was doing life, so he had plenty of time to wait. I further explained it was not fair for me to miss part of my break because of these ungrateful inmates.

Mr. Allen agreed it might not have been fair, but that was okay because life was often unfair. He also asked if there was anything else because several customers at the counter were waiting for law books. First of all, everyone knows that life is not fair. If it were, I would not be locked up in this prison. I would be at home with my girl waiting on me, hand and foot. Another time he said, *it rains on the just as well as the unjust,* and *you reap what you sow.*

What? That does not even make sense. Later an older inmate told me the last two quotes were from the Bible, only confirming my suspicions; the guy was a nutcase. One day, he told me that since I had so much time to complain, it must mean I did not have enough to do, and maybe he should assign additional duties to me. I stopped complaining after that; it never did any good anyway.

While working at the library, I read that the Bible and related books outsold all other publications each year. But I still did not put much stock in all that stuff. I mean, it says you are not supposed to steal.

Everybody steals - bankers, insurance companies, people on Wall Street.

One day Mr. Allen was overheard talking to a colleague about rumors. The prison was fueled by rumors, and some were quite vicious. You will never guess what the librarian had to say on that subject. He quoted his pastor, Reverend Gerald Harris. According to Harris, what people said or thought about you was insignificant. The important thing is what God knows about you. And, according to Mr. Allen, God knows everything, which means God knows about all the crimes I committed, including the ones on which I escaped justice.

I cannot afford to believe any of this; I would have to spend all my time on the lookout for a car ready to knock me down the block. Or maybe a tree will fall and take me out; the possibilities are endless. Besides, if I were to embrace this way of thinking, I would have to change my whole way of living. Who wants to do that?

One day a clerk came across the pay scale for all state workers, which is public information. When we saw his meager salary, we laughed and began bragging about how much more money our careers paid than his; and he went to college. But at least one inmate was lying because I knew him from the hood. Before coming to prison, he lived under a bridge using unwashed hubcaps for plates and his fingers for eating utensils. Coming to prison improved his standard of living. He got a roof over his head, a bed to sleep in, and three meals per day. I suspect that a couple of others were lying as well. They were always bragging about having money but would pick up cigarette butts off the ground to smoke instead of purchasing cigarettes from the canteen.

But I did not lie. I could make more in one month than the librarian made in six, and I didn't have taxes taken out and did not have a long commute. I did not make that much every month, although I did a couple of months each year. True, I carried a gun and exchanged gunshots occasionally. That was what one of those library books called an occupational hazard as was getting shot. I mean, it's a cold world. One must take the good with the bad and the bitter with the sweet. At least that was what Mr. Allen was always saying.

A week after I got fired from the library, I was on the yard pondering my fate. You see, getting dismissed from that library assignment was a big deal. My credit earning status changed because of being unassigned. It meant I was not receiving a day off my sentence for every day I worked. My sentence almost doubled.

Further changes also came with my current status. None were good. Now I would be last for everything, including chow release, yard release, and day room use. I no longer had an income; thus, I would be using state issue soap, tooth powder, and so on when my current stock ran out.

As I sat thinking upon these things, I suddenly noticed things were about to get worse. I saw those fools - jailhouse lawyers - approaching from three different directions. All three appeared to have *shanks*.

I once had a cellmate who explained how to fight three guys successfully simultaneously. He explained the first thing to do is protect your back. He explained you needed to get your back against a wall and keep it there for protection from the rear. Second, decide which two you are going to fight. Choose the two who present the most danger and realize the third guy will attack at will. Accept that you will be on the receiving end of his assault. Third, kick the bigger of the two in the nuts as hard as possible to take him out. Don't worry about losing points for unsportsmanlike behavior. You are not on a television boxing match, and you are not fighting for a championship belt. You are fighting for something far more important; your life, and you do not want the fight to last 15 rounds. Often when the other two see the big guy go down, they will slink off. It takes the fight right out of them. They will not like the new odds. The odds will still be in their favor, but they are cowards. They prefer three to one or four or five to one.

If both continue to fight, get behind one, grabbing him by the neck with your arm choking the crap out of him while using him as a shield from the other guy. Remember, you do not want to go the distance. The longer the fight, the higher the odds are that you will lose.

Unfortunately, my former cellmate did not cover how to successfully fight three guys with shanks, so I disregarded the first part of his advice and adopted the latter. I ran straight to the yard shack, looking for the sergeant. They did not give chase. They did not want to fight, only to chase me from the facility. At least, that was my conclusion as I look back on the incident. I located the sergeant and informed him I could not program safely at this facility.

I went to the hole pending transfer to another joint. The transfer took place seven months or so later. This is where I ran into the would-be landscaper. So, I was stuck in a cell 23 out of every 24 hours awaiting transfer for seven or eight months. I was in this mess because of that librarian and those other fools. Why can't people find the courage to admit they are wrong and accept responsibly? If those clowns had been at the chapel as agreed, they would have their books, and I would still have my library assignment, rolling in dough, not having to start over at a new joint. Losing that job was a significant setback. I could have run a lot of scams from there, banking big bucks. Then I got a brilliant idea; I decided to open my own *jailhouse law firm* upon transferring.

So, I got to the new joint and headed straight to the library at the first opportunity. I talked to the librarian named Washington. I offered to volunteer until a job opened for me. Washington asked to see my ID Card and said my name looked familiar. He went into his office and returned with a piece of paper. He and Mr. Allen were friends, and Mr. Allen had called ahead and given him the 411. That man snitched me off. What's up with that? He should mind his own business instead of going beyond his duties, making life difficult for me. That is the story of my life. Bad luck follows me everywhere I go. People like Allen went out of their way to cause me problems. I came to this joint hoping for a clean slate.

Things seldom worked out for me. My string of bad luck started at birth. See, I did not have a proper upbringing. My mother did not know what she was doing or even how to be a good parent. It started with my role as a class prankster, continually disrupting it because I enjoyed the attention. Whenever the teacher, psychologist, or principal would send notes home about my behavior, my mother would rush up to the school and scold them, not me. She would allege the teacher did not know how to teach. The psychologists needed to go back to school, and the principals did not know what they were doing, period. There were never any consequences for my actions. Then one day, an interesting thing happened. I found it difficult to follow what the teacher was talking about; I couldn't do the work. If I had paid attention in class, things would have been different. I then decided it would be better to be known as the *bad child* instead of the *dumb child*.

So, my *bad* behavior intensified, and my mother never challenged me, just the school. Eventually, I found myself in a school for troubled children, which caused my *antisocial behavior* (school officials' terminology) to increase. That was not my fault either. I had no choice. To stand out in a class of troubled children, I had to create the most trouble. So, you see, my upbringing was suspect. Not only was I the victim of bad parenting, but I also did not receive a proper education. Again, that was my mother's fault. Soon I dropped out of school and began running with the *wrong crowd*, ending up in a place I never expected to be, in prison. Most people do a stint or two in the State Youth Authority before receiving a prison term; thus, they know what to expect. I came straight to prison at a young age.

When I got to prison the first time, my test scores required an education assignment. I did not want to go to school, but the counselor said my choices were to sit in my cell for 22 hours each day or go to school. I choose the school. After all, I knew that if I disrupted the class enough, they would realize their error and change my assignment. I only had to decide on the type of disruption. I suspected it might be more challenging to stand out in this school for the entire student body had behavior problems. Before formulating a disruption plan, I decided to check things out for a week, and I am glad I did. This school was different. The school had guards with billy clubs - a heavy wooden club - for self-defense walking among the *students* waiting to bash someone's head in and guards on the roof with guns looking for someone to shoot. On the first day of my second week, a new inmate entered the classroom and sat in the seat the teacher assigned.

During the third period, I sensed something was amiss. I looked around and saw the new kid glaring at the teacher - who was somewhat attractive - while fondling himself. The teacher told him to *knock it off* and continued talking. The inmate continued. He had everyone's attention and was disrupting the class, the same thing I planned to do but not in this way. The teacher stopped talking and looked at him. The inmate sat there smiling while continuing his activity. The teacher did not give him a note to take to the principal or vice-principal or send him to the psychologist. She left the room, activating the emergency alarm system on her way out. The students sitting near the troublemaker moved away. Within seconds one could hear the thunder of pounding feet. About 20 guards entered the hallway as the teacher pointed out the offender a minute later. She did not utter a single word. The officers rushed into the classroom, knocking over a couple of desks in the process, and grabbed the inmate, threw him to the floor, placed him in restraint gear, and dragged him out of the education wing. Homeboy lost control of his bladder on his way down the stairs.

That was the way they dealt with disruption. They did not send you to the principal or call your mother. Instead, the cops run into the room and start bashing heads. I decided right then not to seek attention in this school. Somehow the attention thing suddenly lost its appeal. These people were crazy.

Weeks later, when I saw someone get shot, I resolved then and there to follow the rules. At least obey the regulations that could get a person shot. A person on the street can at least run from the police and maybe even escape. In prison, there is no place to run or hide. The joint is full of walls, bars, and gates. A brother does not have a chance. Life is just not fair.

As you can see, the deck has been stacked against me my entire life. I have yet to catch a decent break. Misfortune both precedes and follows me. Something always happens despite my very best efforts when things start looking up. Any reasonable person can see it is not my fault. I was not raised right and never received a decent education. I guess I was just born under a bad sign. At least that is what Big Mama said.

POSTSCRIPT:

Proverbs 22:6 advises the reader - the parents - to "Train up a child in the way he should go...." It appears that at least some of the adults in the young life of this man attempted to set him on the proper path. His parents have some degree of blame for failing to follow up. At some point, a person must take responsibility for their actions and adjust their behavior and way of thinking. Proverbs 11:5b warns the reader, "But the wicked will fall by his own wickedness."

CHAPTER 10

The case of the pornographic books

*M*y efforts to replenish the 'Fine Arts' section of the General Library Collection encountered some unexpected headwinds.

This story is about the return of my Warehouse Adversary in another relentless assault. Although the new Supervisor of Education (an African American male) may have been the intended target. There were rumors that dark forces were channeling their energy against him. I may have been a by-product of these efforts.

I thought my battle over book purchases was over. But unfortunately, I was wrong; it was not.

It was late February. While much of the country was experiencing record levels of snow, tons of ice, and low temperatures, spring had come early to California's incredible Salinas Valley. The hills were green, wildflowers were in bloom, and it had been near 70 degrees every day for the past five days.

I worked the late shift that day. I slept late and enjoyed breakfast at a sidewalk cafe in the beautiful City of Seaside before heading for work. I let the top down in my car to better appreciate the great weather. I took a leisurely drive down Highway 68, connecting to the 101 and on to the prison. I was in a good mood, a positive place, or as positive as one could be before entering a state prison, even for just a few hours.

I arrived at the prison, parked, put the top up, traversed the sally ports, and entered the main corridor. *Sally ports are two gates separated by a certain distance and are where a truck (or person) will come into the first gate. The first gate is shut behind them, the truck (or person) is checked for contraband or potential escapees. The second gate is opened, and the truck (or person) continues.*

I was about to enter the library when I encountered Mr. Parham. He invited me into his office and informed me the Supervisor of Education wanted to see me as soon as possible. Mr. Parham further explained that Mr. Lee had received a complaint about a shipment of pornographic books currently in the warehouse that I had ordered. I was puzzled. That is until I entered Mr. Lee's office and saw two of the books in question. At first, I was astounded, then I started laughing. Mr. Lee was not amused, but then he seldom was. I guess it was the pressure of his job. He began questioning me regarding a recent purchase order as he read from a memo, "These books contain pornography, weird pornography…smut… and fat naked women."

Mr. Lee explained his poor mood was partly due to his plans to leave early that day but had to remain on the grounds per the warden's request. The warden was concerned about a memorandum from the warehouse stating the librarian had ordered filth for inmate consumption. The inmates already had perverted minds. Did I think the inmates needed additional materials to feed their perversions? What were you thinking? We have a responsibility to the taxpayers of this state to be prudent with allocated funds.

I left his office and returned minutes later with a copy of the 'R' volume of the World Book Encyclopedia. I opened my defense with the admission that I was at a severe disadvantage. I explained I knew absolutely nothing about pornography and even less about smut. But this I do know. Reproductions of the portraits found in the books on his desk are also available in encyclopedias and fine arts sections in public libraries. In addition, this encyclopedia set is in every elementary school in California. But, not wishing to mislead him, I suggested he visit any public library in any area and see for himself.

Furthermore, these pictures are reproductions of originals located in famous and excellent museums all over the world. When the average person thinks of the *Musee du Louvre* or the *Musee d'Orsay*, they think of places of culture and art, not smut or pornography. I acknowledged that one never knows the thoughts of another. Some may go to museums searching for smut to enjoy and suggested such visitors represent a minority of those visiting museums. I picked up one of the books in question, which opened on a reproduction of a painting of a woman just days away from giving birth. While it looked like a photograph, it was a reproduction of a painting. I pointed out the minute details down to the individual hairs. *This artist had incredible talent.*

"When your boy sees this," I said.

"My boy?" he asked.

"Yea, the one in the warehouse."

I said that he sees fat, but others see a woman about to give birth. However, I will take him at his word if he says he sees smut. When a person's mind is in the gutter, he will see filth when awake, and dream pornographic dreams when asleep. I suspect that one can conjure up smut images when he sees a dog chasing a cat, a woman riding a horse, and everything else in between.

Where your boy views pregnancy as weird fat, others see beauty. I admitted to a lack of medical training. However, I had reason to believe that most pregnancies result in a certain amount of weight gain. The supervisor conceded the point that many women experience weight gain when pregnant.

I handed him the *World Book Encyclopedia* opened to reproductions of paintings by the Flemish artist Peter Rubens, born 1577. I pointed out that Rubens was one of Europe's most celebrated artists during the Baroque era. I noted the fleshy curvaceous women portrayed and suggested nothing was weird about being more substantial than the average size. Some women, considered by many to be among the most beautiful women in world history, were curvaceous. I am glad he did not ask for examples, as I did not have any in mind. But I know this statement is true.

I again noted this set of encyclopedias is available to elementary school children via school and public libraries throughout California. While some inmates act like immature children, the Great State of California had determined they were, in fact, adults, including those in their teens. We work in an adult prison. Thus, in the eyes of our great state, each incarcerated inmate was deemed appropriate for adult legal proceedings and placement in an adult correction facility. Did I understand the supervisor correctly? Does the supervisor of the education department believe that images readily available to eight-year-olds were too sensitive for hardened criminals? If that was the case, I found the argument less than convincing. However, I understood weak arguments are sometimes the only ones a person can offer.

If his boy wanted to eliminate his version of porn from American society, I say, *have a go at it.* However, he should start with elementary school age, not adults. He should go to all the local school boards and demand eliminating all the smut-filled encyclopedias and other materials that his enlightened mind found inappropriate. I agreed we had an obligation to be frugal with all available resources regarding public funds. I suggested that the continued employment of this man was inconsistent with this goal.

Mr. Lee glanced at his watch. It was time to leave for his meeting with the warden. He grabbed the books, including the encyclopedia, and we left his office together. I returned to the library while he continued up the corridor to the warden's office. Minutes later, an emergency count was called, and all programming, such as education, library, and yard activities ceased. All inmates returned to their housing units.

Two teachers dropped by to find out the status of my *smut books*. After informing the two I was waiting for Mr. Lee's return, the discussion turned to other matters. Moments later, Lieutenant Williams saw the three of us sitting in the library and knocked on the door. He stood in the doorway and stated he did not wish to come in but only bid us farewell as the following day would be his last. The lieutenant informed us he had received an emergency transfer to a prison in the Central Valley closer to his home.

We convinced him to join us for at least a few minutes, long enough to explain about the emergency. Finally, he entered the library and shared the following:

He came to Soledad State Prison when he was promoted to Lieutenant two years ago from the Central Valley. He did not want to disrupt his family by relocating everyone to a new area. So, he came alone, shared a house with several others, and went home on his days off. The strain of living apart the past two years was difficult and came to a head several weeks ago. It was so bad that he requested a demotion to sergeant due to an opening of this position at his prior institution.

The problem came to light when he was home on his days off two months ago. It started as a typical weekend. As was the case on most Fridays, traffic was heavy. He left work and headed toward the Central Valley via Highway 101 to Highway 156, then Highway 152. Traffic was still heavy when he reached Pacheco Pass. He stopped for a cup of coffee at *Casa de Fruta* and walked around a bit to stretch his legs. Traffic did not thin out until he reached Highway 5 in the Central Valley. The bottom line was that it was late when he arrived home, and he was exhausted.

Although still tired, he got up early the following day, stumbled into the kitchen, and poured a cup of coffee. He heard his wife say something about *family day* to their son before the son abruptly left the room. His wife explained his son wanted to go somewhere with friends, and she informed their son that the family would be spending the day together. Moments later, a slamming door got his attention. He looked up at his wife and asked, "Did he just slam the door?"

His wife nodded sadly and said, "Yes, he does that all the time."

"What?" I was still sleepy, but the door slamming woke me up. "I will take care of that right now."

His wife became concerned and asked what he was planning. He told her not to worry, to have a seat and some coffee. I assured her that boy would never slam another door in this house. I decided it was time to handle things the way my father did. It was time for me to start running my house the way my father ran his house and treat my sons the way my father treated his sons.

"I got some tools and burst into his room." At first, his son looked annoyed but appeared frightened when he got a good look at my face.

I looked into the mirror and saw my father's face. The face I saw when he had a belt or stick in his hand getting ready to tear into my behind. For a minute, I was frightened too. We all laughed.

I took the door off the hinge, explaining it appears that the responsibility of having a room with a door was more than he could handle. I also told him this was the first step. If I conclude he could not handle the responsibility of having a room, the next step will find him moving into and sleeping in the garage. If any doors in this house needed slamming, I would slam them.

We all laughed again, and someone asked if his father had torn into his behind very often. He replied that it was *often enough*. But according to his father, he enjoyed getting his butt beat because all he had to do to stop the discipline was stop *acting a fool*. Sometimes the father would call it the *cause and effect thing*; you do that, and I will do this, bam.

Other times his father would refer to discipline as a tennis game. "The ball is in your court. Any time you choose to send it over the net, I promise to return it with vigor." In response to the question, "Did you ever stop acting a fool?" More laughter erupted. He answered, "Yea, I am relatively bright. It took a minute to two, but I got the message." Someone said, "...your father sounds like a hard man." To which he replied, Yea, you remember that James Brown song, 'Papa Don't Take No Mess?' That's my Daddy, 'cept for the drinking part."

He returned to the kitchen and told his wife their son would not be slamming his room door anytime soon. He was still in the kitchen finishing his coffee when the gardener entered the yard, giving him a brilliant idea. He went out, talked to the gardener, wrote him a check, and told him to return in two months.

He returned to his wife and canceled the trip to the lake. He informed her the family would be picnicking in the backyard instead. His wife told him he must be nuts. The boys did not want to hang out in the yard. He explained they would not be *hanging out* but engaging in hard physical labor. As for him being *nuts*, she was correct. He was past being *nuts*. He was downright *crazy*. He was so *crazy* he did not care what the boys wanted and called them into the kitchen. He told them the family would spend the day working in the backyard. When his older son asked about the gardener, he replied, "Why should I pay a gardener when I have a door-slamming son who can work for free?" The family spent several hours doing yard work before breaking for a late picnic lunch.

When asked about the emergency, he replied, "The crisis did not become apparent until the following Sunday at church." The pastor spoke from a familiar passage from Saint Mark 8:36, "What good is it for someone to gain the whole world yet lose their soul?" He talked about things that communicated little to me before turning to something that did.

The pastor said many people spend their lives climbing the ladder of success only to find that the ladder was against the wrong wall twenty or thirty years later. Instead of spending evenings and weekends at work, they should have been home with their family. As a result, they become estranged from both their wives and children. This statement spoke volumes to me. I glanced at my wife and could tell that it communicated the same to her.

What was I doing away from home if my son was disrespecting his mother in my house? Was he acting out at school? What if he gets stopped by the police and disrespects them? They might arrest him, bash his head in, or even shoot him. I began looking into a transfer to a prison closer to home. However, none had an opening for the position of lieutenant. So, a few weeks later, I requested a demotion and an emergency transfer to a prison in the Central Valley.

Mr. Banks was an Adult Basic Education II teacher. He asked, "Wait, let me get this straight. You are taking a demotion based on something a preacher said?" Mr. Banks was a non-believer, and he could not understand why people went to church and donated a portion of their salary.

The Lieutenant smiled and said, "If you think that's crazy, listen to this. The chief deputy from my prior prison called and said an opening for lieutenant was coming open in a few weeks and offered me the position. So, I am not taking a demotion after all."

Minutes later, the Lieutenant bid us farewell. We wished good things for him and his family. I glanced at the clock and noticed that although he had said a great deal, he had been there less than five minutes. He talks fast.

My colleagues drifted back to their classrooms, and I started gathering circulation figures and further information for the monthly report.

Forty–five minutes later, Mr. Lee called and said, "You can pick up these books." When I entered his office, he had a rare smile on his face.

"What happened?" I asked.

"Not much. I thought about what you said. I told the warden, my job was to run the educational department, and *my boy*, as you say, was appointed to work in the warehouse. I showed him the pictures in the encyclopedia and suggested that I do my job and let others do likewise. The warden agreed. We spent most of the time discussing other issues. I voiced several concerns the warden promised to investigate. The warehouse will deliver the books later this week."

POSTSCRIPT:

Many spend years pursuing things of limited value, while neglecting more important areas of life with immense long-lasting importance. When Lt Williams realized that his 'ladder was against the wrong wall' he made the necessary adjustments. The Old Testament Book of Exodus 20:12 commands us to 'Honor thy father and thy mother.' We are also commanded to give 'honor' to whom honor is due. Parents represent our first 'authority figures.' If a child learns to 'honor' his parents, then honoring others in authority follows naturally in most cases at least.

CHAPTER 11

The party animal

This story is about a chance meeting of two acquaintances. They did not realize it at the time, but they met on a road called 'Disaster' which led directly to state prison.

The story highlights the dangers of causal, spontaneous contacts. Contacts that are best avoided.

Several years before my career in corrections, Jose and Lee had a chance encounter at a liquor store somewhere in Los Angeles County. The two had met while both were inmates at the county jail a year or so before. Their paths had occasionally crossed after their release. They were not friends per se but rather friendly acquaintances.

On the day Jose and Lee met, Jose was on the city transit heading to his sister's apartment and decided to get off about a mile before to buy some liquor. He happened to go into a liquor store where Lee was buying liquor of his own.

Lee offered Jose a ride in exchange for a beer. Jose purchased a case of beer, and the two shared a beer on the drive and a couple more beers while they sat in front of the sister's apartment talking.

Jose viewed this chance meeting as a good sign due to a problem he faced which he thought Lee could solve. Jose's dilemma was quite simple. He had an invitation to a party but lacked transportation. He could have used the city transit again but didn't want to roll up to the set – party on a bus. That would not be considered *cool*. While the two were drinking beer, Jose discreetly checked out Lee's wheels. While not in the best shape, it appeared capable of making the trip.

It would have been wise for Jose to remember the circumstances that brought Lee to the attention of public safety officials. Lee believed strongly in the death penalty. Not for his misdeeds, of course, but for the transgressions of others. His feeling on this subject was so intense he was willing to administer it himself over what most people consider minor offenses.

The case that brought Lee to the county jail when the two met involved an issue of *respect,* or perhaps *disrespect,* is more accurate. A driver had deliberately run over a puddle of water, splashing dirty water on Lee. The driver was laughing as he aimed his auto toward the pool of water soiling Lee's clothing, so Lee knew it was deliberate. The driver stopped laughing when he saw Lee's gun and quickly fled the scene. Lee went into the street and attempted to fire his weapon, but it wouldn't fire because the gun jammed. The driver quickly turned at the corner, and Lee was unable to administer street justice.

This incident occurred in a commercial section of the community among dozens of people. Someone contacted the police, and Lee was apprehended.

According to Lee, this driver was a nut. Lee felt a solid obligation to teach this driver - and others like him - a lesson and spare others the indignity he had suffered. Lee did not understand why no one realized this or appreciated his service for humanity. Lee did not expect a medal or anything - only a little understanding.

Another mistake on Jose's part was letting Lee attend the party with high expectations. Jose promised the gathering would include good food, quality liquor, and loose women. Lee loved parties but had concerns about not being Hispanic. Jose correctly assured him that would not be an issue.

I once heard a story about a little boy who attended a birthday party. Something upset the little boy at the party, and he responded by urinating in the punch!

At this party, Lee became upset. Much like the little boy, Lee overreacted. What he did was much worse than ruining the punch. The party was in full swing when they arrived. Lee immediately noticed the lack of hard liquor and complained to the host. The host kindly explained that wine and beer were all he offered. Everyone was encouraged to bring a bottle if their preferences extended beyond these.

The food was quite good, and by all accounts, Lee enjoyed a great deal of food and alcohol. It wasn't long before Lee appeared to be under the influence of alcohol after consuming more than his share of both.

After getting his *grub on*, Lee was ready to dance. Perhaps the problem was in his approach. Most ladies do not appreciate a vulgar or derogatory greeting. According to books on etiquette, one is to be respectful when requesting a lady's hand to dance. Or maybe Lee came across as lacking good breeding or taste. Or perhaps it was something else altogether. In any event, there were no takers. No one wanted to dance, at least not with Lee. The host's sister asked Lee to dance, but her husband cut in when Lee started groping.

The evening soon ended, and they called the last dance. Lee went from girl to girl extending an invitation to continue the party at his place. Again, there were not any takers. Upon leaving a party, as described by books on etiquette, one must thank the hostess for an enchanting evening followed by a handwritten note a day or so later. Lee did neither. Instead, he started yelling a bunch of words, most of which contained four-letters. He also called for his friend to hurry if he wanted a ride home.

As Lee approached the door, he took the facial expression on someone's face as disrespect, a significant offense. Lee continued to the car and returned to the party minutes later with two things he did not have before: a pistol in his hand and a bulge in his trousers. One was as large as the other. One witness later told investigators she became frightened when she saw the gun. Still, when she saw the subject was sexually excited, she became seriously frightened.

Lee did not shoot anyone and purposely fired into the ceiling to his credit. He could not understand why the police made such a big deal about things, like kicking in his door several hours later while he slept. One would think they were after someone on the FBI's most-wanted list or something. Sure, he came close to hitting a sleeping child in the upstairs apartment, but how was he to know? The child was not hurt and that was all that mattered. One officer kindly stated that Lee's lawyer would explain things later and said, "We are just the police. We arrest people. We follow orders. Right now, our orders are to arrest you. You will have your day in court soon."

Lee's day in court resulted in a sentence of seven years to life. Killers get less time than that, as do robbers. Life is cruel. Lee transferred to Soledad State Prison and became assigned to the central library in his eighth year of confinement.

Before coming to Soledad, Lee had a Board of Parole Hearing. The Board noted that the mental health department had placed Lee on medication he refused to take. The Board also stated that Lee failed to take responsibility or express remorse for his crime. Based on these factors, the Board decided he was not suitable for parole consideration at this time.

In his own defense, Lee explained the gang he belonged to did not allow members to take psychotropic medication. Besides, his alleged crime lacked victims, so why was he even in prison?

On the first day of Lee's library assignment, my lead clerk suggested I keep a close eye on Lee and said, "Everyone knows he's a nut, so they cut him a little slack. But you had better keep a close eye on him anyway."

Lee was a quick study. I explained his duties and told him he was in charge of the library's science fiction and western/cowboy sections. I informed him of my expectations, which included all books should be in their proper place, leaving six inches on the end of each shelf. The books should also be lined up evenly with the edge of each shelf. I emphasized that each book needed to be in the proper place, to be easily located by our customers.

Lee only had one question. "Who are the customers?" I explained that our customers were inmate library users.

He dismissed this with a wave of his hand. "Inmates are not important, Mr. Allen. You need not worry about them."

"Be that as it may, I expect the books to be in order and lined neatly on the shelf."

To which he replied, "No problem, boss."

The library was closed his first day, and he worked quickly and quietly with little supervision. The following morning within 30 minutes of opening, I heard a commotion coming from his area. I investigated and overheard him explaining to customers they had to checkout each book they picked up.

One customer explained he wanted to see if he had read that book. Another customer wanted to see if the book was interesting. Lee explained that all westerns are the same. He knew this because he read three or four of them over the years. "If you read one, you have read them all." Thus, per Lee, it didn't matter if one had read a particular title.

His advice was to *reread it*. Lee further advised that the story plots were interchangeable. "Some bad dudes come to town, screw things up, and get gunned down by the good guys. That's it, Homes, end of the story."

According to Lee, it was all make-believe and a complete waste of time. Sometimes there was a girl and sometimes not. But if there was a girl, she always ran off with the good guys.

Lee explained, "The bad guys got nothing coming. Just like real life."

I summoned Lee to my office and explained the official library policy. A customer could look at 100 books before deciding which ones to check out. It's called *browsing*.

Lee listened politely. "Maybe on the streets, they call it, how do you say *browsing*, but here in prison, it is called *disrespect*. You want the books on the shelf in alphabetical order. You want the books even with the shelf's edge. You want six inches between the last book and the end of the shelf, and I did all of that. But these fools put books back every which way. That is disrespect to you, the library, and me."

I had Lee cut out pieces of cardboard, color code each piece, and provide cardboard to each browsing inmate. When an inmate picked up a book, he would leave the cardboard on the shelf. Thus, he would know where to return the book if he chose not to check it out. That system helped, but Lee still felt it was disrespectful and a complete waste of time. After all, the books were all *make-believe,* and the inmates only came to the library because they were in prison. According to Lee, none of them went to the library while on the streets. Per Lee, half of the inmates had never even heard of libraries prior to coming to prison, and the other half had heard of libraries but could not explain the concept if their life depended on it. He repeated, "They only come in here because they are in prison. If they were truly interested in going to the library, they would have stayed on the streets. Unlike him, they came to prison by choice."

Previously, Lee had expressed respect for only parts of the library collection: the college section and the inmate law library. Lee indicated these sections contained helpful information. While general fiction was a complete waste of one's time, science fiction was even worse, if that was even possible. I pointed out that sometimes events depicted in science fiction become a reality. Men went to the moon, and perhaps ordinary people might experience space travel one day.

According to Lee, people were never going to travel or live in outer space. "With respect, Mr. Allen, if you want to believe that stuff that is up to you, I do not believe that man ever went to the moon or even went into space." We agreed to disagree.

One day I noticed Lee typing fast and furious, *in between customers*, often ripping the paper out of the typewriter tossing it and inserting another piece. I asked what he was doing. He said he was working on a proposal to enhance the library's operation. For several days in his spare time, Lee worked on his recommendations, almost getting into a physical altercation a couple of times when a customer requested assistance. Finally, he completed the project and left it in my office with a promise that his proposal would make my life less stressful. I accepted his document and graciously thanked him for his devotion to duty, diligence, and unsolicited advice. He said he was looking forward to discussing the matter as soon as possible.

Briefly summarized, his document advocated discarding all newspapers, magazines, and fiction books popular with the *lowlifes*. After all, if they were interested in such things, they would have stayed on the streets. Unlike himself, most came to prison by choice. He suggested retaining and expanding the law library, all nonfiction materials in the general library, and the college section to include highly complex, specialized, and difficult to understand science books. Simply put, he advocated having a collection with limited appeal to the general inmate population. His rationale for these changes included a single factor: the inmates studying the law, and the college students were earnest. They were quiet and did not waste their time with *that make-believe stuff*.

The inmate workers could run everything. But the best part was the librarian could relax and not run to the door every 15 minutes because an inmate wanted to check out *some useless book*. We would not have any, so the inmates would stop coming. The librarian could spend most of his time drinking coffee, relaxing, and just show up every day.

The following workday, I called Lee into the office to discuss his plan. I started by thanking him again for his efforts. However, I pointed out the plan's obvious flaw: very few inmates would come to the library - just law and college students. Lee looked disappointed. That was the whole point. I could come to work every day and relax, kick back and chill out. The intelligent people, those lacking interest in fiction, never caused trouble, were respectful, and always put the books back correctly. And frankly, he was surprised I had never thought of this before, a change he would have enacted his first day of employment.

"You seem intelligent," he said to me.

I tried a different tack. The Department of Corrections expected the inmate library to contain material of interest to the general inmate population. By following his suggestions, library usage would drop dramatically. Lee shook his head sadly.

"Mr. Allen, you don't get it. Nobody cares about inmates. No one is going to check. At my last joint, I knew a guy who spent four years in the first grade. No one came to check why this guy was still in first grade. No one questioned the teacher. Even so, if someone asked the teacher why the inmate was still in the first grade, all she had to say was *because he's stupid*. That's all you would have to say. The suits aka the supervisors only care about your reports. The court mandates the law library, and you will keep that part. That is the only thing anyone will check. If someone did come and ask why fewer inmates went to the library by some weird chance, all you have to say is we have an excellent library.

The books in this library are also in some of the country's leading colleges and university libraries. The fact that the prison inmates are too ignorant to understand the books and not interested in expanding their knowledge would not be your fault."

I could see we were not making progress, so I suggested returning to this issue in a day or two. Fate, however, intervened. Lee was transferred to the North Facility due to an altercation with another inmate in his housing unit.

I never saw him again.

POSTSCRIPT:

Proverbs 13:20 states, "He who walks with a wise man will be wise. But the companion of fools will be destroyed." In other words, it should be the goal of all of us to seek the company of wise people and avoid those who are foolish and quick to anger. Jose should have avoided Lee, and Lee should have found a different group of inmates with whom to interact. Lee thought he was helpful with his proposal to improve the library's operation. However, he approached the issue from a selfish position and not with the welfare of the general inmate population. He thought I should think along the same lines, doing what would, in his mind, be best for me.

CHAPTER 12

The case of the sleepy lover

*S*ometimes, staff members get caught up in the heat of the moment and engage in actions with unforeseen consequences. This story is about a small-minded man. A man whose plans seldom extend past the next six-pack of beer. An annoying, irritating man whose actions caused a staff member to snap. This is his cautionary tale.

Luther was a small-time criminal. He had never made big plans or attempted a big score. For him to cheat someone out of a couple of dollars was a reason to celebrate. He never invested much effort in planning his criminal activity. If Luther were honest, which he was not, he would say his plans failed more often than succeeded. When his crimes made the local newspaper, it would be a line or two in the trivial section, only on a day with limited news. But that was to change soon. Very soon!

The day started like most of his days. He got up late in the morning, lacking plans as he did most days, just taking things as they came. He was a go-with-the-flow kind of guy.

Some people roam a neighborhood picking up trash, while others search for cans and bottles. Luther did neither. Luther walked the city streets with criminal intent. He was always on the lookout for opportunities to commit crime. This day Luther spotted a partly open front door of a house on his daily walk. He looked around to see if anyone else was around. Not seeing anyone, he proceeded to the porch and looked through the window. Still not seeing anyone he knocked on the door and waited for a response. When nothing happened, Luther entered the house through the open door. He reasoned that he was not *breaking in and entering,* just *entering.* He grabbed pillowcases from a closet and filled one with a lamp and other loot.

When Luther was convinced that he had taken everything of interest, he left it all by the front door and walked upstairs. While searching for additional loot, he felt someone looking at him and discovered an elderly woman in bed visibly shaking with the covers pulled up to her chin. Luther felt a stirring in his loins. He walked over to the bed, disrobed, and jumped in. At least in his mind, the two made tender, passionate love. Twice. Luther could not believe his good luck. Two criminal opportunities on the same day and the same place! And he took full advantage of both.

As Luther considers himself a gentleman, he asked the elderly woman if it was *good for her too.* She had the presence of mind to assure him it was, in fact, terrific. An exhausted Luther smiled, turned over, and fell into a deep sleep. His sleep was full of dreams of the financial schemes he would run on his new friend. Things were looking up. It was turning out to be a good day indeed.

As Luther lay sleeping, the victim eased herself slowly out of bed and ran butt naked, as fast as her 82-year-old legs could carry her, to a neighbor who called 911. The victim was still shaking as she sat in the kitchen wearing her neighbor's robe, sipping tea, waiting for the police. She explained her tale of anguish to the police officers when they arrived minutes later.

When she got to the part of the man, Luther falling asleep, the police officers rushed to her house, where they found Luther sound asleep. What happened next is in dispute. According to Luther, he was awakened when a police baton made contact with his head several times. He also claimed that after being placed in hand and leg restraints, he was tossed headfirst down the interior and exterior stairs. He claims to have woken up after the billy club first contacted his head, and when he tried to protect himself, he received head and arm injuries. The police denied these allegations.

In the police report that followed, the officers described how they gently woke the subject and spoke kindly to him. They also reported the suspect was considered *dangerous* and required hand and leg restraints. However, they denied using a compliance tool and tossing him down the stairs. The officers did acknowledge that subject suffered moderate injuries in attempting to negotiate the stairs while in leg restraints and losing his footing, thus explaining the injuries. The report also explained they advised Luther to be careful on the stairs. However, he failed to heed their advice. The officers also claimed to have made a significant but unsuccessful effort to prevent him from falling.

Luther accepted a plea deal. This deal included a guilty plea to several crimes he claimed to lack knowledge of. Still, Luther was not overly concerned about pleading guilty to additional crimes since the sentences were concurrent. Besides, having more convictions on his record increased his gangster image. The fact these additional convictions could hinder future employment prospects did not concern Luther. He had no intentions of ever looking for a job. The police department also benefited in clearing back cases, so it was all good.

Luther arrived at Soledad and received an assignment to the central library as porter/janitor. As an inmate, he was a problem employee due to his laziness, being late for work assignments, and complaining about everything. The bright spot in Luther's life was the female correctional officer assigned to his housing unit. Three days each week, the officer undertook a count of inmates in his housing unit. Each time the officer passed his cell to count, she would find Luther, without clothing, fondling his genitals.

She would order him to stop, but Luther would laugh and tell her what he wanted to do with her. One day in frustration, the officer shared this problem with her housing unit sergeant, with whom she was having an affair. That he was married did not matter because she was also married.

The sergeant, a man of action, jumped up, grabbed his taser gun, and rushed to Luther's cell. In hindsight, that proved to be a mistake. The sergeant should have sat her down in the office and provided a rule violation report form for her to complete.

Instead, the sergeant dared Luther to *show me what you showed her*. Luther was unaware of the taser and proudly exposed himself. Compliance with this unlawful order was a mistake on Luther's part because the Sergeant lacked legitimate reasons to examine Luther's genitals.

The sergeant whipped out the taser like he was Marshall Dillon, at high noon. (Only the Marshall never shot unarmed men, at least not on television.) When the sergeant fired directly at Luther's genitals inmates several housing units away could hear his screams.

The sergeant knew the Department of Corrections policy requires personnel to file a report documenting a 'use of force incident.' It is unlawful to provide false information on such reports. The inmate must also undergo a medical examination with an account from the medical department verifying the injuries. In this situation, the use of a taser violated policy. The inmate was inside his assigned cell, not engaged in illegal activity, and did not pose a threat to the sergeant.

The sergeant's report stated the incident occurred outside the cell and said the inmate threatened prison security and failed to comply with a lawful order. The sergeant also found several *witnesses* to falsify supplementary reports. It might have helped the sergeant if the medical staff had manufactured their statements, too, although this did not occur.

As it happened, Luther's medical examination report and the sergeant's report were completely different. Inmates contacted the media, elected officials, and family members. The press carried stories about inmate abuse. The Department of Corrections Headquarters sent a team to the prison to investigate.

Under intense questioning, the sergeant's conspiracy fell apart, and participants turned on each other to get a better deal, like avoiding arrest or remaining employed. Luther accepted a six-figure settlement negotiated by his attorneys.

Luther finally hit the big time. His story was on the six o'clock news and covered by several prominent newspapers across the state. Plus, he got paid big time. For the first time upon release from prison, the inmate had more than two dollars.

True to form, Luther was penniless, had wasted the six-figure settlement money, and was back in custody three years later, on new charges. But what a time he had!

POSTSCRIPT:

Proverbs 12:15 says, "The way of a fool is right in his own eyes. But he who heeds counsel is wise." A foolish person is not concerned nor considers the ramifications or consequences of their actions. Luther was not one to seek or even express interest in obtaining wise counsel and experienced predictable results. Proverbs 11:27 also says, "He who diligently seeks good finds favor. But trouble will come to him who seeks evil."

CHAPTER 13

Grant's tomb

A group of students comes to the inmate library for the first time. This story is about a prison class field trip when an Adult Basic Education Level II class (reading level 4-6 grade) visits the library.

Eleven months into my tenure as a senior librarian, I posted a note on the bulletin board in the teacher's lounge announcing the availability of classroom visits to the library. A prison field trip! Not a long excursion, just a short walk down the corridor to the opposite end of the education wing to a place many inmates had yet to experience - the library.

The following week, Mrs. Ford approached me and requested a visit for her Adult Basic Education II Class. We discussed our expectations and scheduled a time for the classroom visit. I expected her class to be on their best behavior, and she wanted the visit to be a learning experience. Mrs. Ford and I hoped the inmates would come to view the library as a pleasant place to spend time. We were both realistic enough not to expect the inmates to consider the library *cool* but hoped it would become a place they could go without embarrassment.

I arranged for a few library inmate workers to make a short presentation on the library to break the ice. I also planned to introduce several essential reference tools, including Current Biography, Who's Who, the World Book Encyclopedia, and the World Almanac. I wanted the classroom visit to be a fun learning experience, so I developed a short quiz requiring the use of these tools. I did this to satisfy the learning component and hopefully provide the inmates with previously unknown but intriguing information.

In drafting the questions for the short quiz, I had specific reference tools in mind and composed a simple, straightforward question to start the quiz. A question with an obvious answer to build their confidence in using the reference tools - a softball question. At the same time, I did not want the quiz to be too challenging and turn the inmates off from going to the library. I hoped to demonstrate the library could be a thought-provoking place and planned to offer those who completed the quiz their choice of a magazine from the discarded magazine pile.

The quiz included the following questions:

- *Whose portrait is on the $5,000 bill?*
- *Whose portrait is on the $10,000 bill?*
- *Where was the first Super Bowl held?*
- *What is the address of a particular leading pop singer, a woman, (whom I shall not name here)*

As suspected, the last question generated a great deal of interest - most likely marriage offers by those able to locate the information. I did not bother to tell the class that the home address would not be listed, or that the pop star would not read their mail.

Mrs. Ford's class arrived at the library on time and took their seats in the reading room. The library inmate workers gave their presentation and spoke about several reference books, the type of information each contains, and various newspapers and magazines. None of the class members had visited the library before, or at least none raised their hands when asked. I spoke for a minute or two and told the class their visit would start with a quiz. Some students expressed disappointment their field trip included a quiz but perked up when I mentioned the free magazines.

The inmates were quiet, polite, and attentive, and no one had any questions. Some of the inmates worked diligently in groups, whispering among themselves, while others worked alone. After I complimented Mrs. Ford on how well behaved her class was, she beamed with pride then I retreated to my office to work on a project.

After about 30 minutes, I returned to the reading room to check on the inmates' progress. I expected everyone to be halfway through the quiz and the brighter ones to be close to completion. That was not the case. The quiz forms were blank, and none of the students had answered any questions. Most were still on the first question; the one I assumed everyone would answer without using a reference book - the softball question. The question they would correctly answer within seconds of reading. I anticipated they would read, respond to, gain confidence, and move to question number two.

Several students decided the *softball* question was too complicated and moved on to question number two, then number three, which proved to be as tricky as the others. All the questions were beyond the capacity of the entire class to answer. I was more than shocked - I was flabbergasted.

And what was the softball question? You guessed it - *Who is in Grant's Tomb?*

I gave out the magazines anyway.

Mrs. Ford appeared quite disheartened at her class' performance. She escorted her well-behaved, but uninformed class, back to the classroom, knowing her job was secure.

I overheard one of my inmate workers say, "That poor lady has a lot more teaching to do." The other inmate worker agreed and said, "Yes, they will be in that grade for a long time."

Postscript:

Zechariah 4:10 says, "Do not despise these small beginnings, for the LORD rejoices to see the work begin...." King David did not start out in a palace but rather as a shepherd tending sheep in a field. He was faithful in each assignment God gave, eventually becoming the powerful King of Israel, defeating all who came against him. Several of Mrs. Ford's class members became ardent library users and completed the requirements to obtain their high school diploma.

CHAPTER 14

The dog that was not there

*T*he main character of this story is a young man whose zeal for his mother and sister lead to incarceration. He was the victim of a one-sided relationship. A relationship where one party cares more about the ties that bind than the other party. It is about a very young man who came to prison. In my view, his crime resulted from his deep concern for the well-being of his family. A one-sided concern that was not shared by all family members.

A couple of years before I started working at Soledad, the youngest inmate worker I came to know was on a path leading to prison. I will retell his story based on his file and conversations between us.

For as long as he could remember, it was just the three of them, mother, sister, and himself. Since he was six years old, it had been that way - he was now 16. He does have vague memories of promising to take care of his mother and older sister - promises he made to his father before he died. He had always looked after them as best he could. After all, he was the man of the house. Someone had to look after them, and it fell on him. He was all they had. There was no one else.

The three of them were close. Well, maybe not as close now as before. In recent years, the sister would make remarks about his appearance to her friends - snide, unkind remarks. But that was just her way. She never meant anything by it. After all, it was only the three of them. They only had each other, except for her friends when she was small and her boy-friends when she was older. Like now!

She often found guys with severe issues, serious problems. Things that were important to others when looking for a mate, she found unimportant. It was a small thing to her if a guy she made plans to marry was unemployed or even unemployable. Take this last guy before the one who caused the latest trouble. He could not hold on to a job even if he was chained to it. He could be bound to a job hand and foot and still lose it. He never saw it coming. According to his account, he would be working hard on the job when he would get called into the supervisor's office to sign some papers. The next thing he knew, security was escorting him off the premises. Oh, and they all said the same thing; something about checking with the unemployment office for possible benefits.

The sister understood this new guy fell short of perfection. However, according to her, we all do. She acknowledged the new guy was vain, violent, a liar, did drugs, sold drugs, was mean-spirited, abusive, manip-ulative, greedy, selfish, and dishonest. According to the sister, he was okay other than all of that. After all, no one is perfect; we all have issues. Suppose she waited for someone without problems. If she did, she might always be alone.

When he asked her to move into a new apartment with him, well, she jumped at the chance to take things to the next level. After all, it was a charming apartment, and they were starting their life together. She had a job, although his position had fallen by the wayside a few weeks earlier. Thus, it was only fair that she paid the deposit and the first month's rent.

So, they moved into their first and only apartment. The couple needed furniture, and since the sister had the job, the couple went down to the furniture store, and the boyfriend watched as she signed the papers. The furnishings arrived the next day while she was at work. He explained it was good he was not working as someone had to be home to take care of housekeeping, such as receiving purchases and turning on the power. Things were not good, but okay for a few days, then they had a big fight, as lovers sometimes do, and he threw her out of the apartment. So, she returned home, and once again, it was just the three of them - mother, brother, and sister.

Two things happened a week of two later: the rent was due, and the couple got back together. The mother began to suspect that the two things were related. The daughter explained to her mother that she could not contribute to their household expenses that month as the lovers were back together. The daughter reasoned they should be together because she still had two years of furniture payments to make. However, a couple of weeks later, they were arguing again. The daughter returned to the family home with bruises and a fat lip.

At first, she had refused to leave the apartment she and her lover shared, even after the first couple of injuries. The fat lip changed her mind and the possibility of losing a few teeth. It's not like the teeth would grow back, and she was a bit young for false teeth.

Before she left, he demanded and received partial funds to cover the cost of running the household. He made it clear he expected additional funds on her next payday. He told her the furniture payment was due soon in case she had forgotten. The daughter explained to the mother that she could not contribute to the family expenses in the coming month because of obligations, much like previous months. The mother found this unreasonable and said that the boyfriend was taking advantage of the daughter.

The daughter disagreed and said her man was experiencing a difficult period, and all he needed was kindness and understanding. She needed to be there for him. At the very least, the mother countered that bringing some of the furniture on which the daughter was making payments, to the mother's home would be appropriate.

Feeling caught in the middle, the daughter agreed to go to the apartment and pick up a few items as the family's furniture was in poor shape. A new piece of furniture or two would perk things up a bit, so they agreed to go over to the apartment and bring back a couple of lamps.

When the two arrived, the boyfriend was busy. He had company and did not let them in. When they explained the purpose of their visit, he assumed they had lost their minds or thought he had lost his. He said if they expected him to sit around in the dark, they were crazy. Besides, this was not his first rodeo. Today they would take the lamps; tomorrow, something else, and next, they would show up with a moving van and clean the apartment out. Before long, he would not even have the luxury of sitting in the dark. Without furniture, he would be standing around or lying on the floor in an apartment without lights. Next, the sheriff would be at the door to kick him out for non-payment of rent. Before long, he would be once again depending on the kindness of friends, which never lasted very long. Most people refused to open the door when they saw him on the other side. Soon, he would be back on the streets searching for a place to stay and perhaps having to settle for a suitable bridge to provide a roof over his head.

The mother saw the boyfriend beginning to channel Mike Tyson and dragged the daughter out of harm's way. They left without the lamps, and the daughter left sporting new bruises while the mother was unscathed because she saw the writing on the wall in time. After the pair reached safety, the mother suggested contacting the police. The daughter countered that a minor misunderstanding between two people in love was no reason to involve 'the man'.

Several weeks and payments later, the daughter began to question the extent of his love for her. While she thought of him often, he only seemed to think of her when it was time to pay the bills. So, she called a family meeting, during which they decided to rent a van and collect all her belongings. By so doing, he would realize she was serious, and he was about to lose *his good thing*.

It is not clear why the family thought this was a good idea or that he cared about losing her. Yet, according to police reports, that is the course of action they took.

Sometimes people should leave well enough alone and be content with current gains. At this point, the lover boy should have apologized for all misunderstandings and graciously let them take whatever they wanted. Violence was not only unnecessary but often ended badly.

In the Old Testament story of *David and Goliath*, the giant was aware he was about to engage in a fight. He was completely unaware he was about to enter the last battle of his life, a battle that he would not survive. He expressed contempt for the teenager and his weaponry. It would have been far better for *Goliath* to apologize for insulting *David*, his people and withdraw. The giant was unaware the teenager had fought bears and lions and returned home with trophies. *Goliath's* head and sword were two of the trophies the teenager would collect that day.

Like the giant, lover boy had contempt for the group facing him. He thought he was in the prime of his life. He was completely unaware that the remainder of his time on this earth consisted of minutes, not hours, days, or years. The lover boy slapped the sister.

After seeing his sister assaulted, the brother pulled out a gun. He threatened to shoot the lover boy if he touched his sister again. The lover demanded to know what the brother was planning to do with that *little pea shooter* and threatened to take it and shoot everybody.

With that, the not-so-bright lover advanced toward the brother and attempted to take possession of the pistol. A struggle ensued, the gun discharged, a bullet flew from the weapon's barrel and entered the chest of the lover boy, resulting in fatal injury. Lover boy slumped to the ground, clutching his chest, with a surprised look on his face. Meanwhile, the bullet exited the boyfriend's body, hit the side of the building, ricocheting in a slightly different direction, and hit the mother, who fell to the ground screaming.

The sister saw both her mother and the man she loved, who was slapping her minutes ago, go down. The sister stepped over the mother and rushed to her man, screaming, "Baby, baby, baby." With his eyes wide open, *Baby* took his last breath, still looking surprised. The commotion caused nosy neighbors to open their doors.

The sister informed all present, "My brother did this. My own brother shot my man. He killed my man." There was no concern for the mother expressed or exhibited. Someone called the authorities. The brother saw the handwriting on the wall and decided it was time to get out of *Dodge*. He left his mother, sister, and lover boy behind, departing for the unknown.

When the police arrived, the sister attempted to provide a statement. However, she was so distraught over this 'unjustified shooting' that she was taken to the same hospital as her mother and given drugs to calm her. The police began interviewing the neighbors as the mother and daughter were on the way to receiving treatment, and the brother was on the run.

Two days later, the sister went to the police station to give a formal statement. She explained her mother and brother had never liked or accepted any of the men in her life. The men were never *good enough*. She suspected the real reason was her mother and brother were jealous. Before her brother killed her man in cold blood, she dated four men, and the family had found fault with all of them. It did not make sense to her because she considered them good men.

When detectives enquired into the whereabouts of the former boy-friends, she explained one was in the county jail awaiting trial. Another was in county jail awaiting transport to the state prison, and the other two were already in the state prison. The detective suggested that per-haps her family members had her best interests at heart. He further indicated that people engaged in criminal activities might not be the best group from which to choose friends. She disagreed and explained they were accused of petty crimes and were innocent. She knew they were innocent because they all told her they were. Besides, they were in state prison and county jail, not the federal prison where the serious criminals go.

The authorities developed a different take on the events based on their investigation. They had the benefit of reviewing the boyfriend's arrest record and information regarding his prior prison terms, about which the daughter was clueless. This was in addition to police reports already on file and interviews with her mother and others.

The sister maintained that her family members were jealous of her relationship with her man. She said she could relate to the line in an Aretha Franklin's song, *I don't want nobody always hanging around me and my man*. The sister also claimed her family was continually coming around. They were always attempting to get between the two lovers. However, the sister maintained the couple was happy, in love, and devoted to each other, and he was a good man. The police knew otherwise.

The brother eventually surrendered to the authorities, and received a sentence of 15 years to life. Even though he was only 16, the judge determined he was ineligible for the juvenile system; thus, his legal pro-ceeding occurred in the adult criminal system.

He was transferred to Soledad State Prison from the reception center. He received a work assignment to the central library several months later. Before the brother reported for work, I received a call from Officer Herrera, his housing unit supervisor. She called to give me a heads up regarding my new inmate worker and informed me he was, "Just a kid, a bit immature, oh, and he pretends to have a pet dog." She explained the building staff also pretended the dog existed, but I should feel free to do what seemed right.

As I stood in the corridor for the morning release the following day, I had no problem spotting my new employee. He was the only inmate in the corridor holding an imaginary leash attached to an imaginary dog. He handed me his ticket assignment with his free hand when he reached the door. That is to say, the hand that was not holding the invisible leash. I instructed him to sit down, and I would be with him shortly.

When I called him into my office for an initial interview, he came across as both polite and intelligent. He introduced me to his dog, named *Boy*. The dog was so well mannered, I had forgotten he was there. He understood my expectations but had one concern. He feared that *Boy* might escape from the library during a scheduled unlock. I guess he was afraid that *Boy* would figure out the unlock schedule and bolt out of the library as soon as the door opened.

I explained the library's policy regarding pets; they are not welcome. However, since *Boy* appeared to be well behaved, I was prepared to make an exception. My current duties take up most of my time; thus, I could not be responsible for pets. Instead, I suggested he secure *Boy* to a fixed object whenever *Boy* was not under his direct supervision. That answer seemed to satisfy him, and we moved on to other subjects.

The days turned into weeks, and the weeks turned into months, and my new clerk settled into his job. Then, one day, I realized he did not appear to have his dog, so I asked if *Boy* was sick. He shook his head sadly and informed me that *Boy* escaped via a small opening under the fence while they were on the yard. *Boy* enjoyed chasing squirrels but always stopped at the barricade. This time he went under the barbed wire and continued the chase. It happened a few days before. I said dogs generally know where they live and often find their way back home. I told him this to cheer him up. He agreed but noted his dog would face immense challenges due to the numerous locked doors between the yard and the housing unit.

Around this time, he began requesting permission to take law books back to his cell. I also noticed he had become friendly with the law clerks and often consulted them during his free time.

Time passed by until one day I received a notice informing me he was unassigned from his library position pending transfer. I called him into the office, and he explained the courts had reduced his sentence due to his writ. Because of the change in his sentence, he was eligible to transfer to a lower-level prison.

Before transferring, he stopped by the library to bid his former inmate co-workers farewell. Before leaving the library, he stopped by the office to say goodbye to me. He expressed gratitude for the library assignment and hoped to find a similar job at the new institution. He was happy about the transfer because he was going to an institution with fewer restrictions and closer to home, making it easier for his mother to visit.

Since he mentioned his mother, I inquired about his family's well-being. He related the following. He and his mother had difficulty accepting the fact that the sister they cared so much about never cared much about them. It was a bitter pill to swallow. His mother fully recovered from her injuries and divided her time between the son, her job, and her church. In her opinion, her daughter threw the two of them under the bus. This opinion strained the relationship the three once appeared to share.

The sister had mourned the loss of her true love for several months. She then managed to pull herself together and entered another abusive relationship. The new boyfriend was on parole for attempting to kill his wife. His now ex-wife had the gall to go out for coffee with girlfriends without his permission.

The new boyfriend's ex-wife had the good sense to file for divorce while the husband was still in the county jail and left the state before his prison release. The demise of that relationship was good fortune for the daughter. She was back in love and happy. According to relatives, this new relationship was the *super-real thing*. She had finally found a substantially good man, and her family was not around to kill him, run him off, or interfere in her business.

POSTSCRIPT:

The New Testament Book of James Chapter 4:14 makes a statement about life. "... For what is your life? It is even a vapor that appears for a little time and then vanishes away." This tells us that life is short and fragile. In Psalm 90, Moses also talks about the shortness and uncertainty of life by comparing life to a blade of grass that comes up in the morning but fades in the hot sun by evening. In verse, 90:12 Moses prays, "So teach us to number our days, that we may gain a heart of wisdom." This is a prayer all of us should pray. Wisdom comes from God. James 1:5 states, "...If any of you lack wisdom, let him ask of God, who gives to all liberally...."

The boyfriend should have earnestly prayed to God, asking for wisdom (as we all need to do). Had he done so, it is doubtful that his life would have ended this way and as soon. He would not have been living off of, and taking advantage of people. The mother and her son needed the wisdom to let the sister/daughter go her own way.

CHAPTER 15

Stories behind the
transition to prison

O ver the years, prison law library patrons - the inmates, expressed frustrations and discontent with all aspects of the criminal justice system. According to these inmates, the judges, prosecutors, and the police were biased and worked in tandem to violate their rights. Many inmates of color believed that the police department's role was not to *protect and serve* but *harass and control.*

When considering the origins and history of American policing and my personal interactions with police, I found myself relating to some of their concerns. Criminal justice students learn that modern police departments in this country imitate English policing departments, which came to the East Coast in the 19th century. While true, this is only part of the story.

Policing in slave economy states evolved from the system of slave patrols. The purpose of these patrols (comprised of White men, some volunteers, and some paid) was to enforce slavery-related laws and regulations. They had the power to stop and question any Black person to determine if they had permission to be wherever they were. They could demand documents such as passes or papers declaring that they were not members of the enslaved class of Africans. In published reports, some patrol members were not above supplementing their income by taking and destroying freedom documentation and selling the *legally free* person into a life of bondage.

After the Civil War, these patrols transitioned into police departments with the same mission, monitoring and controlling the behavior of Africans by enforcing 'Black Codes'. One such code required all Black men to be employed. The penalty for unemployment was imprisonment. If a Black man declined to accept a back-breaking job for meager wages, he was subject to arrest by police and imprisonment by the courts. Blacks were only allowed to go to public parks on Mondays. However, on Mondays, a Black person at the park was subject to arrest for loitering or any number of other offenses. In other words, public parks were off-limits for tax-paying Africans in most southern towns.

In some ways, very little has changed. Today private individuals still feel entitled to detain and question African Americans enjoying, for example, public parks, swimming pools, and even walking down the street.

Several years ago, in Florida, a Black teenager returning from the store was stopped by a White man lacking the authority to detain the youth. The teen was visiting his father. The vigilante, however, determined that the teen did not belong in the neighborhood based on his color. With full knowledge that he had done nothing wrong and had every right to continue to his father's home where he was staying, the teen resisted being detained. A confrontation ensued, and the teen, who did not have a weapon, was shot dead. Police declined to arrest the vigilante until public outcry demanded action. When a jury of the vigilante's peers found him *not guilty*, many on various media sites celebrated. One popular media outlet claimed that race was not a factor in this incident and that people *get into fights all the time*. They blamed the *liberal press* for turning the incident into a *race issue*.

A year or two ago in Georgia, three White men determined that a Black jogger did not belong in the neighborhood. They jumped into their vehicles, chased him down, and shot him dead while videotaping the incident. Once again, the police declined to arrest the men until the public outcry compelled them to act. *As noted on social media posts, the arrests occurred after the public saw the video, not when the police viewed the video.* A jury found the men guilty. Decent people everywhere felt a sense of relief. In recent years, videos on social media sites depict private citizens attempting to detain or calling the police on African Americans who *do not belong here*. I have been the victim of such calls. Several years ago, I was detained by a police officer who had the uncanny ability to identify 'criminals' from the distance of several football fields. On this particular day, he identified me. He appeared convinced I had criminal intent for being in his town. I lived in the town and had done so for at least 10 years crime free. After producing documentation proving I lived in the town and was a retired peace officer in the Great State of California, he still continued to demand, "What are you doing here? ..." According to the National Association for the Advancement of Colored People website, 65% of the African American population believed they were victims of selective enforcement or targeted because of their skin tone.

I believe that many of these incidents are the legacy of slave patrols. The patrol's primary purpose was to protect White citizens. They accomplished this by controlling the actions and activities of the enslaved. This control included apprehending and returning *property* to the forced labor camps when the enslaved decided they were not *feeling this slave thing anymore* and decided to *escape*. As noted, any White person had the authority to detain and question any African at any time about anything.

CHAPTER 16

Heat-seeking missiles

*T*he following story provides personal insight into the experiences various inmates claimed happened to them. As a Black man, I have been
detained by police numerous times before this story and since. This story is
about selective law enforcement and offers insight into why so many men
and women of color are over-represented within the criminal justice system.

For many inmates, a direct line exists between action and incarceration. However, this line is not as straightforward for others, or so they
claim. These inmates suggest their confinement is primarily due to the
pigmentation of their skin rather than their actions. As revealed by one
inmate, the police officers in his neighborhood *hone in on brothers like
heat-seeking missiles*. By way of explanation, a *heat-seeking missile* is a
weapons' guidance system that tracks and follows targets using infra-
red light emissions. Later in my life, I started referring to this concept as
the *heat-seeking missile* phenomenon.

In my role as law librarian at Soledad, inmates shared their experiences of this nature. While being out with a group of friends, the
inmates claimed the police would stop their vehicle and detain them

for an hour or more for no reason other than being Black or Brown. The police officers would take extensive notes about them, their associates, and their aliases. They would also be searched and photographed before being released. Other inmates told of being picked up by police officers, interviewed, photographed, driven to, and dropped off in a rival gang neighborhood. Here they ran the risk of being assaulted as they attempted to return home. After consulting various legal books, many concluded that such tactics violated their rights.

I found their experiences challenging to believe since most of them were from South Central Los Angeles and none were from South Africa. However, I later discovered that various gang task force units did frequently detain, question, photograph, and search groups of young Black and Brown men. As reported by a television magazine program, the gang task force used these methods to maintain their database of gang-related information. After watching this program, I felt it was appropriate for the gang task force units to question suspected gang members when there are reasons to believe they were engaged in criminal activity. However, I disagreed with detaining, questioning and taking photographs just because of their skin tone. Also, I only had the word of inmates that they were taken to and dropped off on the turf of rival gangs.

In the autumn of 1986, I had an experience that caused me to reflect on this issue. On that autumn day, I was in the City of Salinas. I encountered a police officer who had clearly decided I was on his hit list for the day. Remembering what the inmates had told me, I now know I supplied the heat the missile was seeking. I was at the intersection of John and Main streets and in the process of crossing at the pedestrian lights. I waited for the lights to turn green before attempting to cross. When I was about one-third of the way across, the light turned red. I remember being surprised the light changed so quickly. People crossing the street from the other direction were also caught by the light turning red. I increased my speed and was met by a police officer when I reached the curb. *What happened next made me aware why so many men of color get arrested and account for 80% of the inmate population. Some people refer to this as selective enforcement.*

I had no idea the officer was waiting for me. As I walked away, the officer yelled, "Hey you, come here." His tone was harsh. I looked around and could see he was talking to me. I stopped as he approached. When he reached me, he demanded my identification. He informed me I would be receiving a traffic citation for crossing the street on a red light. In my view, *the police officer detained and cited me for being Black. Because others were engaged in the same activity, no other explanation presented itself.*

I noticed people walking up and down the street while others stopped to observe my interaction with the officer. I informed the officer the light was green when I began crossing the street. However, he just held up his hand while providing my personal information (name, race, and so on) to someone on his handheld radio. It may have been my imagination, but the officer appeared disappointed that I did not have any warrants to pursue.

The officer stated he saw me when I was halfway across the street, and the light was red. I agreed but noted the traffic light had turned red within a few seconds. The officer came close to calling me a liar, stating that traffic signal lights do not change within seconds, and began to write out a citation. By now, several others had joined the onlookers at a distance to view the long-running show of *Cops*.

I accepted the traffic citation but told the officer to wait while I activated the light to show how quickly the light changed from green to red. Once the light turned green, it changed back to red within seconds. To his credit, the police officer appeared surprised and requested that I return the citation. The officer acknowledged the timing of the traffic light cycle did not allow sufficient time for a person to cross the street and requested again that I return the citation.

I refused to return the ticket and expressed fear the citation would be discarded, setting me up for a *failure to appear* arrest. The officer gave me the look one reserves for those amid a mental health crisis. He spoke softly, slowly explaining I could trust him as an officer of the law and that he would not engage in questionable behavior.

I again refused to return the ticket, noting that his behavior was already questionable. *I did not mention he could have detained others but chose to detain me.* Eventually, we reached a compromise. The officer signed his business card, which contained his name and badge number. He wrote the citation number on the back of the business card and the incident's time, date, and location. We made an exchange - the citation for the business card.

I have also encountered similar incidents that could have turned out completely different but for the Grace of God. What if that officer had found a reason to arrest me? Maybe I resembled the description of a *person of interest*. Even though I was innocent of the jaywalking offense, I still risked arrest and having my parked auto towed. This could have resulted in thousands of dollars in storage fees. Due to selective enforcement of this nature, I concluded that many men of color are currently within the criminal justice system.

Shortly after this incident, I saw a leading conservative address this issue on a political television program. The commentator stated the answer was quite simple. There are more Blacks in prison *because Blacks commit more crimes.* As proof, the commentator noted the rate of *Black-on-Black* crime. This statement is not consistent with the available facts. In my view, people use this comment to demonize African Americans. But if one wishes to have an honest discussion of the issues, one must acknowledge that the *White-on-White* crime rate is similar to that for Blacks. Suggesting that African Americans are more violent than other groups, requires one to ignore the numerous wars in Europe and other related atrocities. There have been numerous wars launched by Western powers, resulting in the loss of millions of lives. In addition, European powers launched wars of conquest (resulting in genocide) on continents worldwide.

Various crime studies suggest that people tend to be victimized by family members, friends, neighbors - people they know. In the case of homicide, the spouse is generally the number one suspect until cleared. While the term *Black-on-Black* crime has been in the national lexicon for years, the expression *White-on-White* crime is absent, even though both groups experience similar crime rates.

Some suggest the urban murder rate is a reflection of society's gun laws. Others note that guns do not magically appear in these communities. Instead, someone is producing, trafficking, and selling guns to different factions, profiting from the violence. Instead of bemoaning *Black-on-Black* crime, the criminal justice system should make serious efforts to eliminate the source of illegal weapons.

The Old Testament Book of Genesis tells the story about the death of *Abel* at the hand of his brother *Cain*. God went to *Cain* and inquired about *Abel's* whereabouts. *Cain* pretended not to know. God tells *Cain*, "The voice of your brother's blood cries out to me from the ground." I believe the blood of murdered victims are crying out today. Responsible parties who escape accountability in this life will not avoid punishment in the next. Social status, political power, or wealth will not be mitigating factors. Those who assault and kill peace officers will account for their deeds, as well as officers of the law abusing their positions.

The Book of Numbers, New Century Version, 14:8 tells us, *The Lord never forgets to punish guilty people.*

When presented with a potential problem involving a person of color, too often, the response appears to be unleashing law enforcement resources. Several years ago in New York, someone observed a Black man selling single cigarettes from an open pack. The police responded to the scene, and the *offender* died during this encounter. I realize this behavior must be against some regulation, but it should not be a capital offense. Minor violations become capital offenses most often when a person is Black. Yet many members of the evangelical community claim *all lives matter,* and those who advocate *Black Lives Matter* are racist. This group continues to provide full support to the system that condones these murders.

Thus, many appear incapable of stating the phrase *Black Lives Matter,* much like a high-ranking official in a previous administration. This person self-identifies as a member of the evangelical community. When asked to state *Black Lives Matter* in an interview, this person refused and declared *all lives matter.*

Many members of this community, that is evangelicals, do likewise. In my view, all lives have never mattered to most of this country's population. (Native Americans may have an opinion or two on this subject). All lives matter to God, but not to man. If I am incorrect, and all humans matter to most Americans, then when was this mark reached? At what point did all lives matter equally? At what point in American history did all lives receive fair, just, and equal treatment?

While many components contribute to the devaluation of Black lives, I would like to focus on the role of the media outlets, educational institutions, and the Christian church.

POSTSCRIPT:

After giving this situation of police detention, much thought, I concluded that the police officer did not see me as a person, a human being, but rather as an object. A criminal object that required removal from the streets of the City of Salinas. He could have greeted me in a civil tone as if I was a respectable tax-paying citizen, which I am, but he did not. He could have listened to my explanation of why I was crossing the street on a red light before issuing a citation, but he did not. He could have looked around and noted others crossing the road as I was detained, but he did not. I was the person of color while the others were not. As such, my presence required police attention. I was the one who was different. I did not belong, even though my ancestors on my father's side arrived on these shores in the 1700s and provided free labor for well over a hundred years.

Most of the males in my family served in the military, (with distinction), in wars from World War II to Vietnam and other conflicts - this is more than many congressmen, senators, and a president or two. At what point will White America stop viewing Blacks with suspicion? I am grateful the police officer allowed me the opportunity to demonstrate that the traffic signal timing did not allow sufficient time to cross the street; and that we were able to resolve the matter without going to court.

CHAPTER 17

Do all lives really matter?

M *any people, including members of the evangelical community, claim*
all lives matter and imply that those claiming Black Lives Matter are
racist. The same people even argue that racism does not currently exist, nor
ever existed, or was imbedded in the founding institutions of this country.

This chapter attempts to ascertain the point in American History when
all lives mattered equally.

Some argue racism is not part of the country's foundation. However,
the original text of the Constitution of the United States, various court
judgments, codes, laws, and customs suggest (shout) racism **was** at the
core of the country's foundation. People advancing the argument that
racism never existed are either knowingly making false statements -
known to be untrue - or are misinformed.

There is a dichotomy between the Federal Government's response
to the biggest radioactive spill on Navajo Nation land in Arizona and
the partial meltdown of the Three Mile Island nuclear reactor in
Pennsylvania. This dichotomy screams that all lives do not equally
matter. Both disasters occurred in 1979. The spill on Navajo Nation

land produced more than twice the radiation as the Three Mile Island incident.

The cleanup of Arizona's Navajo Nation land is incomplete 40 years after the event, and the victims failed to receive adequate compensation. This is described in the *YouTube* video, *How the US poisoned Navajo Nation - Vox October 12, 2020*. The cleanup of Pennsylvania's Three Mile Island nuclear reactor meltdown began immediately, and companies provided compensation to the victims.

Some people may say this example is an isolated event, and all lives have always mattered. A brief examination of historical facts suggests otherwise. In the view of some historians, kidnapped Africans first reached this continent in the year 1619 and immediately became enslaved. These forced labor camps (plantations), produced tremendous wealth and put the country on its current path to becoming a superpower. The enslaved people created economic wealth and profits for others, but not for themselves. I think all reasonable people would agree *all lives* did not matter in 1619.

On July 4, 1776, the thirteen North American colonies published the *Declaration of Independence which* states all men are created equal. However, the document's main author, Thomas Jefferson, 'owned' over 600 enslaved people during his life. Jefferson 'owned' enslaved people before, during, and after drafting the *Declaration of Independence*. Several of his enslaved personnel were also his descendants. This document also refers to Native American as 'savages'. Thus, *all lives* did not matter equally in 1776. Not even those that came from the loins of Mr. Jefferson himself!

Even my ancestors did not matter enough to avoid being enslaved.

The Constitution of the United States is the supreme law of the land. Delegates to the 1787 Constitution Convention reached what is known as the *Three-fifths Compromise* agreement over the counting of enslaved people to determine a state's total population. This sum would decide the number of seats in the House of Representatives each state would have and how much each state would owe in taxes. So, the official law of the land stated African people were only three-fifths of a person. However, the total count of African people in each state provided additional representation in Washington, D.C. for that state. Yet, *none* of these additional representatives advocated on behalf of the enslaved, a double whammy for the enslaved. To be clear: slave economy states received additional representation in the federal government due to the number of enslaved persons residing in the 'forced labor camps.' However none of these additional representatives advocated on behalf of the enslaved nor made any efforts to improve their living conditions. The African numbers were included to determine the state's number of representatives all of which worked overtime to make life more difficult for the African. Thus, *all lives* did not matter in 1787, just *some lives*.

For generations, the Native Americans lived in, which is now, Georgia, Tennessee, Alabama, North Carolina, and Florida. On May 28, 1830, President Andrew Jackson signed *The Native American Removal Act*, leading to the event known as the *Trail of Tears*. This law removed Native Americans from their ancestral lands to provide farmland for newly arrived White settlers. Between 1830 and 1850, the Federal Government, via the United States Army, forced approximately 125,000 Native American people to relocate to accommodate this need for additional farmland.

This forced displacement of Native Americans - at gunpoint - sometimes occurred in inclement weather. Many Native Americans lacked adequate protection from the elements and died during this forced displacement. The formerly enslaved people who had escaped and were living among the Native Americans were kidnapped and sold back into slavery. So, *Brown lives did not matter* in 1830 as much as White lives.

Between 1820 and 1860, the production of cotton increased. Eventually, 80% of the global cotton supply came from the southern

United States. The output of this commodity by enslaved labor brought immense wealth to the South. Plantation overseers placed extreme pressure on the enslaved to meet their daily yield. As documented in historical records, some overseers expected each enslaved person to pick 200 pounds of cotton each day.

Professor Carol Anderson, in her book 'White Rage' (page 11) writes that *millions of enslaved people and their ancestors had built the enormous wealth of the United States; indeed, in 1860, 80% of the nation's gross national product was tied to slavery.* Anderson stated that, *in return for nearly 250 years of toil, African Americans received nothing but rape, whipping, murder, the mutilation of families, forced subjugation, illiteracy, and abject poverty.* Yet again, *all lives did not matter* between 1820 and 1860.

Under California's law passed in 1850, neither African Americans nor Native Americans could testify for, or against, Whites. This law did not apply to Asians. In People v. Hall, Chief Justice H. Murray promptly corrected this oversight. The Chief Justice ruled that Chinese citizens or immigrants could not testify against Whites. Hall, a White man, was convicted and sentenced to death for the murder of a Chinese man. Hall's trial included the testimony of several Chinese witnesses. Chief Murray's ruling provided Hall with a *get out of jail and off death row card.*

For clarity, the court ruled Asian witnesses - even to murder - were not creditable enough to testify against a White man in court. So, did all lives matter?

The *Father of Gynecology*, Dr James Marion Sims, made significant advancements in women's reproductive health after years of research at the expense and pain of enslaved Black women. In 1876, Sims became President of the American Medical Association. Sims conducted the bulk of his study on African women without anesthesia. I repeat, without anesthesia! Supporters of Sims claimed the lack of anesthesia was not because he derived sadistic pleasure from inflicting pain on women of color. They claimed it was because of his sincere (but false) belief that Black people did not feel pain. Maybe Sims thought the anguish of women crying during these operations resulted from *playacting*. Or perhaps he thought they were lazy and did not want to contribute to science.

The view that Blacks feel pain at a lesser rate than do Whites persists today. Some history books still imply enslaved people enjoyed toiling under the hot sun for over 12 hours per day without compensation. These false narratives suggest enslaved people were happy and loved their slave conditions. My father's grandmother was born into slavery. She was 15 years old when the Civil War ended, thus freeing enslaved people. She died when I was nine years old. My great grandmother's recollections of this period of her life was far less rosy.

The good doctor Sims did acknowledge some Black women victims experienced agony. At one point, men hired to hold down the enslaved women during these experiments quit due to their discomfort over the women's suffering. The good doctor then instructed enslaved people to restrain the women, which had at least two advantages: the enslaved people could not quit, and they worked for free. After perfecting his technique, the good doctor began treating White women with anesthesia. The good doctor Sims also tested surgical treatments on African children for neonatal tetanus with less success.

So, during the era of Dr James Marion Sims, *all lives did not equally matter*. White women underwent surgery with anesthesia, and Black women were victims of his medical experiments without anesthesia. Dr Sims did not face legal consequences for conducting experimental surgery without anesthesia on Black women, suggesting that *all lives did not matter*. The lack of significant public outcry regarding this atrocity is further proof that all lives did not matter. Some monuments honoring this man fell victim to 'cancel culture,' leading to their removal.

In 1852, Dred Scott entered the Supreme Court of Missouri as a free man and became enslaved during the legal proceedings. For some reason, Scott was unhappy with this outcome and appealed this decision to the United States Supreme Court. The brilliant Chief Justice Roger Brook Taney wrote the court's noteworthy opinion with assistance from the President of the United States.

This case appeared to be a waste of the court's time. The fair, balanced, impartial, and compassionate judge wrote that Scott was not a United States citizen. Thus, this Negro had no business in his court trying to sue a White man. Furthermore, the Chief Justice stated Africans could never be citizens of this great country. The Constitution of the United States did not consider Africans as *people*. Thus, they were ineligible to receive government protection.

In case Scott still did not get it, the Honorable Justice broke it all the way down, writing,

> "*Blacks had no rights* which the White man was bound to respect; and that the negro might justly and lawfully be reduced to slavery for his benefit. Scott was bought and sold and treated as an ordinary article of merchandise and traffic whenever profit could be made by it."

This means that *Black lives do not matter*. The respectable, impeccable, impartial Chief Justice could not have spoken more plainly. The United States Supreme Court ruled that Black lives only mattered as *an ordinary article of merchandise*. Black lives did not matter in the past, did not matter now, and would not matter in the future. This was the view of the highest court in the United States.

A rumor I once heard suggests that the Chief Justice laid aside his papers and spoke from his heart after delivering his decision. The rumor went something like this:

I want to know, who let you up in here dressed like a White man, and did that person know you were attempting to sue somebody White? You and everyone associated with your case must be crazy. You get your behind out of here, out of those fancy clothes, and back to those cotton fields where you belong. The White man that owns you has lost enough money behind this nonsense.

The official court records do not reflect the Chief Justice made the above statement. Perhaps it is just a rumor, after all.

In 1852, a court in Missouri ruled that *Black lives did not matter*. On appeal, a higher court affirmed that Black lives mattered as *articles of merchandise* only and *reduced to slavery for his benefit*. Thus, in 1857, the United States Supreme Court reaffirmed that only White lives matter - along with the Constitution of the United States. Yet, to date, some people still claim the concept of White supremacy was not present in the formation of this country.

On December 1, 1955, Rosa Parks boarded a bus in Montgomery heading home. Instead, Parks rode into the pages of American history via the local jail.

In 1892, Homer Plessy had a similar experience while traveling by rail in Louisiana. The state had enacted a law requiring separate railway cars for Black and White passengers. Although considered Black in Louisiana and all other states, Plessy, seven-eighths White, attempted to travel in a White-only rail car. (After all, Plessy was far more White than Black.) After refusing directions by the police to vacate his seat, Plessy was taken into custody because this grave offense required public safety resources.

The 1896 Plessy v. Ferguson judgment became the legal foundation for racial segregation in the United States. His lawyer argued the state law violated the 13th and 14th Amendments to the Constitution of the United States. The court disagreed, and Plessy was convicted. Jurisdictions focused on the *separate* part of the decision creating different facilities for Blacks and Whites. The fact the facilities were far from equal was considered a small matter. This was considered so minor, the courts did not address this issue until 60 years later.

In considering judgments made by the United States Supreme Court, African blood is so robust that even if a person is just one-eighth African, that person is to be feared and subjected to a marginalized existence.

POSTSCRIPT:

Many people, including some political leaders, claim racism was not part of the founding of this country. One of the most famous documents in American history - the United States Declaration of Independence - states, "...all men are created equal." Yet the document refers to Native Americans as *Indian savages*. Several Native tribes in the New England area fought and shed blood on behalf of the American Revolution only to find that the new country was reserved for Whites after the war. Most were eventually forced out to Wisconsin in 1822.

CHAPTER 18

Backlash and resistance

B lack economic and social progress has historically been met with both backlash and resistance.

This section reviews some of the major acts of violence (massacres) occurring between 1863 and 1923 against African Americans by White mobs. In most cases the victims were not compensated for their loss, nor were guilty parties brought to justice.

Some suggest that the Civil War which ended slavery in the United States is proof that all lives matter. After all, the country went through a major conflict over this issue. However, I propose the real purpose of the Civil War was to preserve the Union; freeing the enslaved people was a byproduct of this effort. In addition, while many were fighting on the Union's side, others fought to preserve the enslaved status quo.

After the Civil War, some 'owners' of enslaved people received compensation for the loss of their *property*. However, after several hundred years of free labor, all the enslaved people received was continued brutality under the Jim Crow laws. These were state and local laws enforcing racial segregation in the southern United States. However, all other areas included various forms of marginalization in some way. After the rebellion, the country squandered the opportunity to confront and defeat racism. A backlash - often violent - has always followed Black progress. Many believe the injustice experienced by African Americans ended with slavery. This argument is inconsistent with the facts. The problems are far more treacherous than just slavery.

For several years after the Civil War, Blacks made social, political, and economic gains before White resentment kicked in. Laws, regulations, Black Codes, Jim Crow laws, voter suppression, police misconduct, and domestic terrorism swiftly eliminated these gains. The Black population soon returned to a position similar to slavery, which did not change until the Civil Rights Movement of the 1960s. The following is a partial list of what some historians consider to be among the worst massacres of African Americans by White US citizens responding to Black progress:

- **1863 New York City Draft Riot.** The Civil War broke out in 1861. As the war progressed, the anti-war media and politicians expressed concerns to working-class White citizens. This included that emancipation of the enslaved would result in competition for employment when the newly freed enslaved moved from the South to New York. Before this period, most European immigrants settled in the northern part of the country due to limited employment opportunities in the South. The enslaved had a monopoly on most of the southern jobs. In September 1862, Lincoln proclaimed his emancipation plans to take effect in early 1863, thus increasing racial tensions. The federal government faced a serious military manpower shortage and enacted a strict conscription law. All eligible men were entered into a lottery but could hire a substitute or pay the government $300 to avoid serving. The newspapers attacked the draft law, which fueled the anger of White workers. Thousands of White workers attacked military and government buildings before moving on to Black homes, Black businesses, and Black people. In addition, rioters targeted White abolitionists, businesses that catered to Blacks, and White women married to Black men. The worst violence was reserved for Black men who were beaten to death or lynched. Some estimates of the number of people killed were as high as 1,000. The New York City draft offered a path to citizenship for the recent arrivals from Europe. However, free Africans were ineligible for citizenship due to their skin tones.

- **1866 New Orleans massacre.** On July 30, 1866, a group of formerly enslaved men and some White men were attacked by former Confederate soldiers, White supremacists, and New Orleans Police Force members. The Black men and their allies were peacefully demonstrating against Black Codes and the lack of voting rights for Black men. Black Codes restricted the freedom of Blacks and forced them to work for low wages. The violence occurred at the site of the reconvened Louisiana Constitutional Convention. The Republication Party of the state had called for the convention as they favored extension of voting rights and opposed the enactment of Black Codes. Some estimated that up to 200 Blacks were killed and 150 wounded. One White protestor and three White convention attendees were also killed. This incident took place in the Bible Belt! The Bible Belt is known for supposedly having a high prevalence of Christian religious beliefs. It is characterized by the high rate of residents who regularly attend Christian Worship services and profess to have strong Christian values.
- **1866 Memphis massacre.** Occurred between May 1-3, 1866 and involved White rioting mobs and Police officers against Black veterans and Black civilians. A shooting altercation between

White police officers, mobs of White citizens and Black veterans of the Union Army occurred. Police went on a destructive binge attacking and killings Blacks, committing robbery, arson, and rape. The carnage included 46 Blacks and two White people killed, 75 people injured, 100 Blacks robbed, and every church and school in the Black community burned. An investigation concluded that competition for working-class housing and employment played a role in this incident. The violence was also a way to enforce social order after slavery ended. This event, along with the 1866 New Orleans massacre, impacted the passage of the Fourteenth Amendment granting citizenship to the formerly enslaved Africans. This incident also occurred in the so-called Bible Belt!

- **1868 St. Bernard Parish Massacre.** As Black men gained the right to vote following the end of the Civil War, White men faced the prospects of losing their voting majority and their way of life. In October 1868, White men in Louisiana's St. Bernard Parish mobilized to suppress the Black vote and regain their role in the community, disrupted by the war, the end of slavery, and Reconstruction. Blacks were dragged from their homes and murdered—the reported number of Blacks killed varies from 35 to over 100. Many escaped by hiding in the cane fields for several days. Brave Black survivors identified several White neighbors as assailants; however, no one was arrested for the murder of the Blacks. Once again, this occurred in the Bible Belt without significant pushback by White Christians.
- **1868 Camilla Massacre.** This was another backlash to the political, social, and economic advances made by Black people. White supremacists carried out this incident to halt and roll back this progress. In September 1868, the Georgia State legislature expelled 28 members because they were at least one-eighth

Black. On September 19, 1868, one of the expelled legislators led several hundred Blacks and several Whites on a 25-mile march to Camilla to attend a Republican political rally. Whites were stationed in storefronts with guns and fired upon the marchers entering the courthouse square. As the marchers retreated, Whites followed for several miles continuing their assault. Another proud moment for the Bible Belt residents, a place full of Christian values but not a safe haven for People of Color.

- **1868 Opelousas Massacre.** On September 28, 1868, an outbreak of violence occurred in Opelousas, Louisiana. A newspaper editor and teacher, Emerson Bentley, was in the classroom when members of the Knights of the White Camellia entered. They beat him for his past support of voting rights and education for Blacks and warning the Blacks about the dangers to the African community posed by the *Ku Klux Klan (KKK)*. African Americans came to his aid, prompting mobs of White citizens to roam the countryside in a murderous rage killing more people, most of whom were Blacks. It was a successful attempt to discourage Blacks from voting. Another high-water mark for residents of the Bible Belt.

- *The KKK is a violent terrorist organization initially founded to target African Americans and, later, many other groups.*

- **1873 Colfax Massacre.** Occurred on Easter Sunday and claimed the lives of at least 150 men. Whatever the numbers slain, all but three were Black. This massacre is remembered as a major event and predecessor to the establishment of the Jim Crow system. It led to the 1875 Supreme Court case (US v. Cruikshank) banning federal prosecution for racially motivated crimes. The massacre occurred amid increased racial tensions following the contested race for governor. When the Grand Old Party (GOP) won and retained control of the state, White Democrats were angry over the defeat and looked for revenge. In Colfax Parish—as with most parishes—White militia was formed to directly oppose the (mostly Black) state militia under the governor's control. The 4,600 voters in Colfax Parish were split between 2,400 mostly Black Grand Old Party votes and 2,200 White Democratic voters. In March 1873, local White Democratic leaders made plans for armed supporters to help take the Parish Courthouse from the Black and White Grand Old Party officeholders. On April 13, Easter Sunday, when most 'Christians' were at church, over 300 armed White men, including members of the KKK, attacked the courthouse building. Approximately 150 Blacks were killed, including about 50 murdered after the battle. Another Bible Belt story.

- **1874 Vicksburg Massacre.** Like most incidents of this nature during this era, the Vicksburg massacre was designed to reassert White supremacy. It is estimated that between 75 to 300 African Americans were killed. A formerly enslaved and Union Army veteran Peter Crosby had been elected Sheriff. A group of White citizens forced him to resign from his duly elected position as Sheriff at gunpoint. He was told that he had a choice. He could either walk out of the room alive or be carried out dead. When Blacks organized to defend Crosby, the Whites attacked, killing so many that the Blacks were forced to flee. The governor's appeals for order had little effect, as did the company of troops the president sent. The president's troops reinstated Crosby as sheriff. However, torchlight processions, military drilling, harassment of Black workers, and the assassination of Black leaders soon drove him from office again, this time for good. This also took place in the Bible Belt.

- **1874 Eufaula Massacre.** In 1874, Henry Frazer was both a Black Republican and Methodist minister. He had spent several weeks canvassing support among sharecroppers. Frazer led 400 Black men toward town to vote on the day before the election. He promised them they would be protected and not to bring weapons. Upon arriving in town, they met another group of Black men in town for the same reasons. Blacks comprised most of the population and had previously elected Grand Old Party candidates to office. That would soon end. Later that day, members of the White League killed an estimated 40 Blacks, wounded 70, and drove over 1,000 unarmed Blacks from the polls. By controlling the polling site, the White League hijacked the elections. It forced all the Republicans out of office, and the Democratic candidates took most offices up for election. This incident occurred near Eufaula in Alabama in the Bible Belt, known for its strong Christian values.

- **1875 Clinton Massacre.** On September 4, 1875, as many as 2,000 Black Republicans and their families gathered for a political rally to enjoy speeches, barbecue, and meet the candidates running for political office. About 100 Whites also attended, including a few Democrats in the nearby town. While a Republican was speaking, shots were fired. When the gunfire ended, five Africans were dead, including two children. Three Whites were dead, 30 others were wounded. Newspaper accounts stated that the Blacks were defending themselves. However, many Whites were enraged that Blacks had the nerve to do so. White mobs shot and killed 50 Blacks in and around Clinton, Mississippi, in the country's Bible Belt. The Blacks were sharecroppers, farmers, unskilled laborers, and other working-class poor.

- **1887 Thibodaux Massacre.** At least 60 Blacks were killed and ended the dream of unionized southern farm labor for decades. After the Civil War, sugar cane workers lived in old slave cabins. They endured the same work condition their ancestors had experienced for the past century. Some growers provided meals but paid wages as little as $.91 per hour in today's money for a 12-hour shift. Instead of legal tender, workers received scrip to be used at the plantation stores, which always had higher prices than the local stores. When the workers attempted to band together and demand better conditions and more pay, many were shot, and their bodies dumped in unmarked graves. The White press cheered the end of the Black union. This incident also occurred in the Bible Belt.

- **1891 Wilmington Insurrection.** This has been labeled the *only successful coup d'état in United States history*. Black voters joined forces with poor Whites and elected Black and progressive politicians to office. Whites began to feel they were losing or had lost their grip on power. A mob of 2,000 White supremacists descended on Wilmington to overthrow the legitimately elected biracial government. The heavily armed mob expelled the elected leaders from the city, destroyed the property and businesses of Black citizens, and killed as many as 300 Blacks. While other violent incidents occurred during this era, this is the only one that included direct removal and replacement of elected officials by unelected persons. Wilmington is situated in North Carolina, which is in the Bible Belt. Another area claiming to have the strong Christian values.

- **1906 Atlanta Race Riot.** The riot took place against the backdrop of a major increase in the city's population—(within 10 years, 60,000 people moved to Atlanta) - stiff competition for employment and the 1906 gubernatorial race. For the first time in the city's history, Blacks and Whites were openly competing in the limited job market. Candidates Hoke Smith the (former) publisher of the Atlantic Journal, and Clark Howell, the editor of the Atlantic Constitution were in a unique position to influence public opinion via their media sites. Both took full advantage of the opportunity. Smith claimed that Black disenfranchisement was necessary to ensure *they* were kept inferior to Whites thus maintaining the current social order. Howell claimed that he (Howell) was the better racist because Smith had past dealings with Blacks and could not be trusted to sufficiently advance the cause of White supremacy. All the local newspapers began reporting unsubstantiated stories of White women being assaulted by Black men which increased circulation. Besides inspiring fear and resentment, this had the additional benefit of increasing profits. On September 22, 1906, all major Atlantic newspapers reported four alleged unsubstantiated assaults of White women by Black men. The accounts were sensationalized and contained lurid details and inflammatory language. These articles inspired fear and the desire for revenge as thousands of White men and boys gathered in the downtown area. The group soon turned into an unruly mob. It began attacking hundreds of random Black men, Black-owned businesses, breaking windows, jumping on streetcars beating Black men and women. It is estimated between 25 to 40 Blacks and two Whites were killed, including a woman who suffered a heart attack upon seeing the mob near her home.

- **1908 Springfield Riot.** In the birthplace of Abraham Lincoln, a race riot occurred on August 8, 1908. An innocent Black man was lynched by a White mob, enraged over the false claim he had raped a White woman. *After the riot, the woman recanted her tale and left town.* This incident resulted in the burning of several blocks of homes and businesses where Black people lived and worked. Two highly respected successful Black businesspeople - Scott Burton and William Donnegan - were also killed, causing great anguish among the Black population. This tragic event gave rise to the legendary social justice organization The National Association for the Advancement of Colored People (NAACP). This tragic event did <u>not</u> occur in the Bible Belt.

- **1910 Slocum Massacre.** On July 29, 1910, near the small east Texas town of Slocum, White men shot and killed eight unarmed Black men. Some estimates of the number killed are closer to 100. The reasons behind this event have not been established. Of the 11 White men arrested, seven were indicted. Eventually, the charges were dropped without anyone being prosecuted. Some definitions of the Bible Belt include Texas.

- **1917 East St. Louis Massacre.** The massacre of St. Louis was a series of labor and race-related violence by White mobs that killed between 40 and 150 Blacks. Another 6,000 Blacks were left homeless. The homes and businesses of Blacks were also destroyed.

- **1919 Chicago Race Riot.** The catalyst for this tragic event was a Black teenager on a raft drifting on Lake Michigan who crossed an invisible line dividing White Chicago from Black Chicago on July 27, 1919.

- **1919 Washington D.C. Riot.** According to published reports, this riot was somewhat unique in that there were more White casualties than Black. Newspapers increased circulation numbers with lurid headlines of Black men sexually assaulting White women. Social Justice organizations wrote letters to the paper warning that potential violence could result from such sensational uncorroborated headlines. However, to refrain from printing such stories would have a negative impact on the newspapers' bottom line, so the stories continued. On July 18, 1919, a White woman married to a White United States sailor alleged she was attacked by a Black man on her way home from work. An allegation she later recanted. The next day her husband gathered a hundred servicemen and began assaulting Blacks. When the police failed to offer protection to the people of color, Black veterans joined together, took matters into their own hands, and offered the protection the police failed to provide.

- **1919 Red Summer.** Hundreds of thousands of African Americans migrated from the Bible Belt to other parts of the country in the early part of the 20th century. The underlying cause for this mass movement was the continuing racial violence - lynching, massacres and targeting Blacks in the south. The Red Summer refers to an outbreak of violence that affected at least 26 American cities all over the country. It was a pattern of White on Black violence that occurred in 1919. Much of the wrath was directed toward Black veterans returning home from World War I in Europe. They were often treated better by Europeans than by White Americans. The Black veteran's expectations of equal treatment after their brave service to the country and generations of enslaved labor were met with hostility. It is estimated that over 100 Blacks were killed. These tragic events occurred inside and outside of the Bible belt.

- **1920 Ocoee Massacre.** On election night eve, KKK members paraded the streets of two Black communities in Ocoee, Florida. They warned that not a single Black person would be permitted to vote. When Black Americans attempted to vote, a massacre ensued, and an estimated 50 Blacks were killed.

- **1921 Tulsa Massacre.** This massacre occurred on May 31 and June 1, 1921. A mob of White residents, some deputized and provided weapons by city fathers, killed Black residents and destroyed homes and businesses in the Greenwood District of Tulsa, Oklahoma, known as Black Wall Street. This area was home to numerous Black millionaires. White mobs killed hundreds of residents, burned over 1,400 homes, burned 35 city blocks to the ground leaving 10,000 homeless, and eliminated years of Black progress in a few hours. Insurance exclusions allowed insurance companies to avoid honoring claims filed by most Black policyholders. One of the factors driving the tragedy was resentment toward the Black prosperity found in block after block of thriving businesses and fine houses in the Black community. The massacre began during the Memorial Day weekend after a Black male teenager was accused of assaulting a White female teenager.

- **1923 Rosewood Massacre.** This was another racially motivated massacre of Black people. The entire town was destroyed during the first week of 1923. This took place in Florida. Before this tragic incident, Rosewood was a quiet Black town. It was a whistle-stop on the Seaboard Air Line Railway. Florida had a high number of Black related lynchings. This trouble began due to accusations that a Black had assaulted a White woman in the nearby town of Summer. A mob of several hundred White men killed over 100 Black men, women, and children. The town was abandoned by its residents and ceased to exist. No one was ever compensated for their losses.

- **Supplementary information.** During the Reconstruction era over 2,000 lynchings of African Americans by White supremacists occurred throughout the southern states. Between 1877 and 1950, 4,400 additional lynchings are documented. Information regarding these (and related) incidents are available in Wikipedia and YouTube channels such as Emory University, Black American History CrashCourse etc. This information can also be found in books, articles and various other media sites.

The public recognition of these events would provide insight to the entire nation regarding the generational trauma still affecting many

African Americans. Yet, laws are currently being passed in over half of the states in the union outlawing the teaching of these events in public schools. In some cases, the same people who decry the removal of monuments to the Confederacy as erasing history, pass laws to prevent fact-based historical accounts from being taught. It is suggested that school-age children may feel uncomfortable hearing such things. *I suspect that the adults do not want to deal with the resulting generation trauma.* But if it makes the young feel uncomfortable, that is why the subject matter should be addressed. Such teaching may help prevent history from repeating these incidents.

Germany addressed its Nazi past without monuments to the Nazi leaders. The country engaged in open discussions of its history and recognized those disadvantaged and victimized by the Nazi regime. Many suggest that recognizing the nation's past misdeeds may cause the younger generation to hate America. I reject this argument. I suggest it will cause the younger generation to develop a more mature view of our society and move forward, not back.

An alternate narrative for not teaching fact-based history suggests that the true agenda of those who fabricated this narrative has less to do with concerns about education, and more to do with maintaining the status quo. The images of George Floyd dying at the hands (or knee) of police resulted in global protests. These protests extended to the country of Belgium where statues of King Leopold II were toppled. The king imposed a harsh and brutal regime on the Congolese people while extracting (stealing) large amounts of natural resources (wild rubber and precious minerals) from the African Colony. The African death toll is still unknown. The rubber brought vast wealth to Belgium. Today it is estimated that the Congo has $24 trillion worth of mineral wealth.

It is suggested some fear that the teaching of historical events today could cause a massive shift in public thinking, resulting in a shift in political power. The public may question the treatment of indigenous populations and the natural resources on their lands. People may question the treatment of 'Third World Countries' and the resources the Western countries take for almost nothing. People in the West may conclude that poorer countries should not have to live lives of desperation in order for people in the West to enjoy a high standard of living. Financial markets do not like uncertainty. Much like the people in power, the markets prefer the status quo.

POSTSCRIPT:

From this partial and very limited view of United States history, it is difficult to understand why some members of Congress claim that racism does not exist; or state the country does not have a racist past or was founded on Christian principles. There is nothing Christian about massacres, thievery, kidnapping, rape or lying about the existence of such events. Those who spout such rhetoric are either woefully ignorant, lacking knowledge, or engaging in deception. Any of these should disqualify a person from public service. At least that is my view. Jesus warns us to be careful in our treatment of the *Least of These*.

CHAPTER 19

Other backlash events

*S*ome people think that slavery was the only hardship Africans had to endure when they were forcibly relocated to the North American continent starting in 1619. The truth is that Blacks have also contended with those in a position to reverse Black progress or inflict pain and suffering. This chapter provides insight into some of these matters.

President Woodrow Wilson

In 1913, Woodrow Wilson (son of a preacher man) - considered progressive - was elected President of the United States and served until 1921. Before entering the White House, Wilson served as Governor of New Jersey and prior to becoming Governor, was the president of Princeton University. As President of the United States, Wilson continued to be a staunch segregationist, reversing much of the progress previously made by African Americans.

While a member of the academic world, Wilson wrote a book titled *A History of the American People.* The book portrayed slavery as a kind patrician institution, with ecstatic workers - the enslaved - and suggested reconstruction victimized Whites.

Reconstruction attempted to improve the lives of formerly enslaved people by granting them the right to vote and other advances. His book praised the Confederacy and the KKK.

Journalist Becky Little reported in the article *How Woodrow Wilson Tried to Reverse Black American Progress*, (History.com, 7/14/2020), the following:

> "During Wilson's presidency, he allowed his cabinet to segregate the Treasury, the Post Office, the Bureau of Engraving and Printing, the Navy, the Department of Interior, the Marine Hospital, the War Department, and the Government Printing Office. This change meant creating separate offices, lunchrooms, and bathrooms for White and Black workers. It also meant dismissing Black supervisors, cutting off Black employees' access to promotions and better-paying jobs, and reserving these jobs for White people."

Before Wilson became President, the Federal Government was one of the few places offering Blacks employment with possible career advancement. Those opportunities ended with Wilson's *progressive* presidency. Therefore, an honest observer would conclude that all lives did not matter during this era.

Sergeant Isaac Woodard

In 1946, Sergeant Isaac Woodard, along with thousands of African American veterans, returned from the battlefields of World War II. While still in uniform, hundreds of Black veterans were victims of mob violence, and an unknown number were lynched. At least one southern Black veteran lost his life for voting. As Sergeant Woodard, dressed in uniform, was returning home to South Carolina on a Greyhound bus, he asked the driver to stop so that he could use the restroom. The irritated driver referred to the soldier as a *boy* before stopping. The decorated soldier informed the driver that he was a man, not a *boy. After all, boys cannot withstand the horrors and pressures of the battlefield and receive medals in the process.*

Upon reaching the next town - Batesburg, South Carolina - the driver called the police. The Police Chief rushed to the scene oozing southern hospitality and Christian charity that many police officers reserve for Black men. The Police Chief pulled Woodard off the bus and beat him. The Police Chief, fulfilling his oath to uphold the law, then plunged his blackjack, which was a short, easily concealed club, into Woodard's eyes, gouging them out. What was Woodard's crime other than to be born a person of color? The Black veteran spent a painful night in jail without medical attention, maybe, because many claim that Blacks do not feel pain. Woodard later reported someone poured whiskey on him and claimed he was drunk.

An organization of 'radical left-wing communist-inspired agitators' came to Woodard's aid. This organization was called the National Association for the Advancement of Colored People (NAACP). These 'revolutionary communist agitators' raised funds to sponsor a speaking tour for the wounded veteran to raise awareness of the plight of Black Americans. A benefit concert co-chaired by Heavyweight Champion Joe Louis (Colin Kaepernick was not the first professional athlete to protest police brutality) included Billie Holiday, Woody Guthrie, and Duke Ellington. God bless all of them. In addition, the NAACP asked actor Orson Wells to highlight the brutal assault on his weekly radio show. God bless Orson Wells too. Due to Orson Wells and others, the town and identity of the Chief of Police became known.

When this information became public, thousands of White Christians flooded the streets of southern cities demanding justice for Sergeant Woodard. Some carried signs stating, *Stop the Lynching* on one side and *All Lives Matter* on the other side. Other signs stated, *Respect the Military*, and *Stop Assaulting Black Vets*. Simultaneously, church ministers preached that Pro-Life includes Black life and all police misconduct must stop.

Unfortunately, that did not happened. That was fiction. These are the facts. Officials in South Carolina did not investigate the incident. Local government and state authorities declined to file charges against the Chief of Police when his identity became public knowledge. In the eyes of many White citizens, the public safety officer - the Chief of Police - had not committed a crime. After all, the Supreme Court had already ruled that Blacks did not have any rights that Whites had to respect. I guess this included the right of sight.

Eventually, the Federal Government filed charges against Police Chief Lynwood L. Shull for violating Woodard's civil rights by subjecting him to a life without sight. The incident took place in the Bible Belt. The Bible Belt is in the southern part of the country where slavery existed. Thus, Chief Lynwood L. Shull faced a jury of his Bible-believing, church-going, God-fearing, evangelical Christian peers. The trial judge J. Waties Warning, (the son of a Confederate soldier), played a pivotal role in the fight against Jim Crow. Although he was unable to influence this verdict, he once ruled that Black and White school teachers should receive the same pay as well as other such rulings. For his efforts, crosses were burned outside his home and bricks thrown through his windows.

Two soldiers from the bus that day, one Black and one White, testi-fied. Both stated Woodard was not drunk, did not create a disturbance, and had not engaged in untoward behavior. The case was not compli-cated. Thus, the jury was not out long. The good decent men of the jury deliberated the issues, considered all the facts, and returned a verdict of Not Guilty within 15 minutes.

When I ponder such matters, I often think of the first Bible verse I memorized as a child, "Jesus wept."

Within hours of the verdict, White church members in towns and cities in the whole southern part of the country flooded the streets by the millions. They were screaming at the top of their lungs, "All Lives Matter" and "Stop Disrespecting the Troops." Preachers quoted Old Testament Prophets from pulpits, shouting, "God requires justice, and followers of Christ should stand on the side of justice." Unfortunately, these large-scale Christian demonstrations did not occur. Even pas-tors disagreeing with this verdict feared the wrath of church members and demonstrated their commitment to biblical principles with their silence.

White Christians were complicit with their inaction, thus condon-ing the evil in their midst. As this all happened in the Bible Belt, one can only wonder what the plight of Black life was like in the secular sections of the country. The Bible warns the reader of the dangers of perverting justice and dishonest weights. In the words of an old Negro spiritual, *Everybody talking 'bout Heaven ain't going there*. Unfortunately, enslaved people found the behavior of far too many White Christians inconsis-tent with biblical teaching.

During President Wilson's presidency, Wilson spoke about a war where the conflict was necessary to make the world safe for democracy. But decades later, democracy was still unsafe for Woodard, his peers, or any African living south of the Canadian border. Hundreds of Black soldiers survived fierce battles of World War II without injury, only to succumb to Jim Crow laws upon returning home. Colin Kaepernick did not disrespect the American Troops. The Chief of Police, Chief Lynwood L. Shull, did and kept his job. The jury disrespected the troops with their unjust verdict. The citizens of the town disrespected the troops by not demanding justice. The entire nation disrespected the troops by not demanding justice for the many African American troops that suffered injustice upon returning home.

In 1948, Reverend Vernon Johns delivered a powerful sermon entitled, *It is safe to Murder Negros*. The Reverend reviewed several stories in the local press involving the recent deaths of two African Americans at the hands of the police. According to police reports, both received gunshot wounds in the back while resisting arrest. The coroner determined that both killings were justified. Johns further noted that a White man had recently received a citation for hunting rabbits out of season. He suggested that Alabama laws offer greater protection to rabbits running wild in the fields of the state than that afforded African Americans. According to the Reverend, one could only hunt rabbits during specific times in the year; however, Black people were always in season.

Dr. Martin Luther King Jr.

In 1963, Dr. Martin Luther King Jr. sat in an Alabama jail cell following his arrest for protesting social injustice in Birmingham, Alabama. On April 12, eight White Birmingham clergymen wrote an open letter responding to the civil rights demonstrations. The clergymen suggested that **if** rights were being violated, rather than demonstrate, protestors should use the court system to address their concerns.

Because, I guess, this had always worked so well in the past. Just ask Sergeant Woodard or the thousands of families whose loved ones were raped, assaulted, and lynched, where neither investigations nor arrests occurred. These ministers were either out of touch with reality or dis-honest and had no right to claim to speak for Almighty God. At least, that is my view.

So, these clergymen were of the opinion the protestors should just walk past Confederate monuments and into the court building - with more monuments - and seek the justice available to all Americans. These were men of the cloth, good God-fearing Bible-believing leaders of the community. Dr. King responded to the letter, arguing that demon-strations were necessary to protest unjust laws and address African Americans' daily lack of justice. Dr. King also expressed disappointment his White Christian brethren had not joined the injustice protest, serv-ing as a bridge to those in power.

The 'Ick' Factor-Criminal Creation

From 1619, when Africans arrived on the North American continent and were enslaved, to the end of the Civil War, to the protests of the 1960s, Black people faced grim living conditions. Faith in God and belief that God would answer their prayers sustained many Black families during this period.

The fact that voting rights, fair treatment in education, housing, and employment required federal legislation, proves that all lives did not matter politically, socially, economically, or educationally. Some lives were more important than others. Some were entitled to fair treatment, while others were not. Some suggest this country did not become a real democracy until the enforcement of the Voting Rights Act, granting Black, Brown, and poor people the right to vote throughout the country. This legislation encountered intense opposition, (which continues to this day), and demonstrates that many did not believe all lives mattered equally.

In my opinion, the conservative United States Supreme Court's gutting of the Voting Rights Act was an unfortunate act for democracy. According to published reports, several states erected barriers to voters of color the day following this ruling. These efforts continue today. Across the country, state legislatures are enacting laws impacting the voting rights of Black, Brown, young, and poor people everywhere. Violence, marginal existence and continued injustice have been the plight of Blacks on this continent since 1619.

As noted, the death of George Floyd at the hands of Minneapolis Police resulted in global protests. Over the years, the Target Corporation (Target) in conjunction with the city's leadership played a major role in the marginalizing people of color in Minneapolis. Target is also one of the city's largest employers. Downtown Minneapolis was undergoing revitalization when the company expanded into that area.

Bloomberg posted an online article titled *How Target Got Cozy with the Cops Turning Black Neighbors into Suspects* on August 25, 2021. According to the article, redlining and racial covenants in Minneapolis kept African Americans from living in specific neighborhoods and acquiring wealth.

> "Black residents faced an outsize chance of arrest and incarceration. This April the US Department of Justice announced an investigation into the Minneapolis Police department for potential patterns of racial discrimination and excessive use of force. Downtown, the worlds collided. The largely White, middle-class Minneapolitans who lived in newly built apartments in the area commuted to work there. They flooded the neighborhood's bars on weekends, irritated with the poor, mostly Black and American Indian people on the streets."

Surveys in the early 2000s found many Twin City's residents felt uncomfortable working and shopping in their midst. It was less about actual safety—violent crime was down—than what Target executives called *safeness*.

A Minneapolis police chief, quoted in a 2010 Police Executive Research Forum report sponsored by Target, used another term: '*ick factor*'.

Following this, city leaders created the Safe Zone program to make the new arrivals feel comfortable. As a result, the Police Department increased the number of arrests to 9,000 in 2009, a 60% increase from 2004. The vast majority of these arrests were for misdemeanors, and 60% of those arrested were African Americans. However, only 20% of the Minneapolis residents are Black. The public safety agencies in Minneapolis targeted African Americans and other long-term residents for police action because they were considered icky by the recent arrivals - similar to the conditions resulting in the *Trail of Tears and the need to create additional space for recent European settlers*.

The Safe Zone program effectively criminalizes the poor, the young, and people of color because of something called an 'ick factor'. The vast majority arrested were not guilty of serious crimes and, as noted, were long-term residents of the area. Under these new laws, arrests and subsequent convictions prevented these long-term residents from returning to the newly created Safe Zone.

The Target organization contributed considerable funding and resources to support this effort on behalf of the public safety agencies and exported similar programs to other cities. There are 50 states and almost 20,000 towns and cities in the United States. Law enforcement's heavy enforcement footprint amongst people of color is a common thread running through all states, cities, and towns. Per published reports, the United States has the highest number of incarcerated individuals on earth. This country contains roughly 5% of the world's population but 25% of the world's prisoners. Could this be related to 'ickyness?' Are people with mental health issues, economically disadvantaged, and people of color victims of the 'ick factor'?

Thus, a person's opinion of the criminal justice system often reflects their interactions with law enforcement agencies. One person may view the police officer as an agent who maintains order. At the same time, another may consider the same officer an agent of oppression.

As noted, the criminal justice system has a disproportionate number of incarcerated Black and brown inmates relative to their respective numbers in the country's population. Most of the inmates, (as previously noted) including White inmates, come from economically disadvantaged sectors of society. In the 1980s, African Americans comprised 11.8% of the nation's population. In Soledad State Prison, approximately 40% of the inmates were Black during my years as law librarian. Could it be that the lives of people of color and people without means are considered less valuable than others?

Studies have examined policing factors in light of the country's racial composition. Some researchers concluded that law enforcement is often applied unequally based on race.

Research documents illustrate how different groups received disparate treatment at each stage of the criminal process, resulting in higher confinement rates for people of color. I suggest this higher incarceration rate is a reflection of the group's status or lack of power. While all lives matter to God, some lives matter less than others to men.

While working as a librarian in Soledad State Prison, the San Jose Mercury Newspaper studied this issue. The newspaper found that when Black and White suspects faced the same offense, the White suspect was often sentenced to less jail time. Officials justified this finding by explaining that White suspects usually have more resources, aka money, or come from good families, aka influence. In many cases, the charges were either reduced or dismissed for the White defendant. In contrast, the Black defendant went to court facing charges on the original complaint.

On November 19, 2018, the Washington Post published an online article titled 'Black Men Sentenced to More Time for the Exact Crime as a White person'. The article reviewed a sentencing disparity study from the United States Sentencing Commission at the federal level. The disparity study titled *Demographic Difference in Sentencing: An Update to the 2012 Booker Report* found relaxing the Sentencing Commission sentencing guidelines allowed racial bias to enter the sentencing process.

In 2005, in a United States Supreme Court case, US v. Booker, federal judges were permitted more discretion in sentencing. With this new discretion, judges gave longer sentences to Black defendants than White defendants for the same crime. Other factors also entered the picture. The study suggested that federal prosecutors were more likely to charge Black offenders with an offense requiring a mandatory minimum sentence. In contrast, White offenders were charged with crimes allowing judicial discretion - another double whammy.

POSTSCRIPT:

Laws, court cases and official government acts all conspire to continue the original functions of the former slave patrols, that being, maintaining and controlling people of color and others that fall within the 'icky' factor.

CHAPTER 20

The media

*T*he media is uniquely positioned to bring social issues and political mis-deeds to the public's attention. While this happens on occasion, all too often - at least on some cable networks - the emphasis is on pushing a spe-cific agenda and not educating the public. Some media sites continuously provide misinformation. This chapter briefly examines the relationship between the media and Black Americans.

In December 2020, the Kansas City Star - a prominent newspaper in the American Midwest, offered a genuine apology to the African American community within its sphere of influence. The Editor, Mike Fannin, revealed that an investigation into the newspaper's past report-ing disclosed that the paper had disenfranchised, ignored, and scorned African Americans since the newspaper was formed.

The investigation uncovered the newspaper had done so with biased reporting regarding people of color. The paper's lack of objectivity started on the paper's first day of operation. The investigation revealed the newspaper had *robbed an entire community of opportunity, dignity, justice, and recognition.* Further, it only included coverage of Black people when there was *suspected criminal activity.*

On December 21, 2020, the Washington Post reported that within a year of the Kansas City Star founding in 1880, all but one of the 150 stories about Black people cast the community negatively. This was usually as murderers wielding weapons, thieves, or accused rapists...Later coverage described Black people as brutes.

This type of media coverage from mainstream media outlets is typical of reporting regarding communities of color. This bias reporting gave rise to the Black press, which commemorates the highs of Black life, laments the lows, and covers everything in between. The Black press coverage is fairer and more balanced towards the community it serves.

Some American media sites continue to spew lies, misinformation and offer false equivalency arguments without consequences. Such actions result in a misinformed citizenry. Due to this misinformation, many people believe that nefarious forces stole the 2020 presidential election denying Mr. Trump a second term.

Many people also think that Black Lives Matter affiliated protestors stormed the nation's capital on January 6, 2021, instead of Mr. Trump's supporters (in spite of texts messages from many members of the President's political friends urging the White House to call off the protest). I can disprove the theory that Black Lives Matter protestors were responsible for this incident.

If Black protestors had injured 140 police officers, erected gallows, while shouting Hang Mike Pence - the sitting Vice-President - broke windows, doors, and trespassed all in a single afternoon, authorities would have called in the cavalry immediately. The Capitol grounds would have resembled the battlefield after General Custer's Last Stand. The protestors would have suffered the same fate as Custer's 7th Cavalry Regiment. Not only would there have not been any survivors, but not a single body would have been left intact; the grounds would have been littered with body parts.

Based on specific media sites, many believe that most of the Black Lives Matter protests were violent during the summer of 2020. However, less than 10% of the 2020 Black Lives Matter protests contained violence, with 25 lives lost - a tragic event, to be sure. These protests took place over several months in various locations around the country.

The January 2021 sedition occurred in a single afternoon, resulting in five deaths. Some people believe these false narratives because of inaccurate media coverage and the lies of political leaders. All media sites should identify false statements immediately. Lies and incorrect information should not be allowed on the public airwaves.

In February 2021, a cable network commentator stated that police did not murder George Floyd. Instead, according to this commentator, Mr. Floyd died from drug use. This statement is inconsistent with available facts, such as the findings of more than one medical examiner and the video witnessed by millions of individuals worldwide.

This same cable network frequently presents false information as accurate. Since most of the people watching this network receive their information from this source, they are unaware of the deception. This example is just one of the many ways lies are distributed to viewers daily. This cable network's coverage of the social justice protests during the summer of 2020 was particularly harsh towards those seeking justice, portraying them as outlaws and criminals. However, its coverage of the January 6, 2021, insurrection was extremely sympathetic, downplaying the violence. On January 6, 2021, *civil disobedience* became a time-honored tradition per this media site.

In addition, other commentators on this network pushed the false narrative that Black Lives Matter protestors attacked the Capitol grounds on January 6, 2021. The cable network also gave airtime to false reports that a previous president was not born in the United States, thus ineligible for the office he held. These were lies. These lies placed the president and his family in danger of harm by unhinged viewers. This outlet also distributed stories politicizing wearing masks and getting vaccines during a pandemic although company policy require those engaged in such reporting to be fully vaccinated.

In summary, this cable network and other media sites push anger, resentment, and hate while opposing policies that benefit its viewers. While such lies produce significant profits for the company, I believe the production and distribution of such programing has horrific consequences for the country. They encourage people not to take precautions during a pandemic causing divisions between families, neighbors, churches, and friends.

POSTSCRIPT:

The Bible asks, "What does it profit a man to gain the entire world but lose his soul?" The money, fame, and access to power may be nice now, but what good will these things do in the next life? I can understand why non-believers live as if life after death is fiction. However, believers know the Bible teaches otherwise.

CHAPTER 21

Educational institutions

*T*he lack of accurate historical information provided by educational
institutions contributes to the divisiveness in American society. This
chapter is about the harmful role played by our educational institutions in
failing to educate society.

Public school districts in the United States frequently fail to address
or include contributions made to the nation's development and the culture by non-Europeans, although this is beginning to change. All too
often, the decimation of the Native American population is minimized.
This is also the case with the impact of slavery on creating the nation's
wealth and the brutal physical and mental toll on African Americans.

Historians refer to the middle passage - the transportation of kidnapped Africans across the Atlantic Ocean - as the largest forced migra-
tion in human history. It was a harsh, savage, and inhumane journey.
Estimations are that between two and four million humans died en
route to America. Most would have to agree that all lives did not matter
during this period.

The reduced emphasis on the brutality of this period is partly due to the booksellers' desire to access the southern market, markets that have a vested interest in downplaying the harshness of slavery. Such revelations would make it challenging to claim enslaved people were happy and enjoyed their slave conditions when so many did not survive the journey.

Such disclosures would not fit the lost cause narrative. This narrative claims the owners were fine people, and enslaved people were delighted to endure hard labor without compensation. Some even argue that the enslaved received free room and board.

I suggest if a person were to work 12 to 14 hours per day, six to seven days each week, and the only compensation received was room and board, it is far from free. I would further suggest this would be among humanity's highest-priced room and board arrangements.

History classes gloss over the obvious contradictory demands of slave-owning colonist seeking freedom from British rule. Yet, simultaneously, the lives their 'slave property' endured was far more severe than anything the colonist experienced.

Some historians believe the living conditions of enslaved people at Mount Vernon - George Washington's estate, were typical of enslaved people during the 18th century in Virginia. According to published accounts, Washington believed his enslaved people were treated well. He gave them just enough food to keep them alive and two sets of clothes each year. As a businessman, Washington felt it was in his best interest to feed and clothe his 'property' as cheaply as possible to maximize profits.

Plantation records document the fact that the enslaved approached Washington on more than one occasion to voice concerns that their meager rations did not last the entire week. Being a kind, merciful man, Washington allowed enslaved people to fish and trap wild animals to supplement their diet during their downtime. This downtime was after working 12 to 14 hours per day, six to seven days each week!

As one of the leaders of the American Revolution, Washington was so enraged over British tyranny, he led the colonies in open revolt. Washington did so while providing only enough food to keep the enslaved Africans under his care alive. He did not dare provide anything extra due to his fear of harming his business' bottom line.

Eventually, at least one female enslaved African decided that working 12 to 14 hours per day, six to seven days each week, was unsatisfactory and escaped. Washington went to great lengths to track her down and demanded her return. Freedom from taxation without representation was his due. However, Washington considered substandard housing, inadequate rations, and the lack of employment compensation for the enslaved sufficient and fair. Public education classes should not gloss over these facts.

The public education system should also examine the impact of slavery on the wages of poor and working-class southern Whites and whether slavery affected employment opportunities for this group. According to the White House Historical Association, many of the early government buildings, including the White House, were constructed with enslaved labor and free Africans. Many of those in the forced labor camps were skilled workers in various trades and in agriculture production. Did enslaved laborers depress the wages of the White working class? If so, it appears the only benefit slavery offered this group was psychological; they were not at the bottom of the pecking order. They had someone to look down on. I would prefer the cash, but then that's just me.

Did the involuntary immigrants take jobs away from *real* Americans and depress their wages simultaneously during this period? This is the era some descendants of these American people celebrate, romanticize, and hold up as their heritage. In the inmate vernacular back in the day, 'what's up with that?' Bigotry harms more than the hated; it can also hurt those harboring hostility. In this case, it may have cost those who hate, legal tender.

POSTSCRIPT:

These are just a few topics all educational institutions should address. A few excerpts taken from a 7th-grade textbook used in Virginia public schools from the 1950s through to the 1970s illustrates my point:

- *A feeling of strong affection existed between masters and slaves…*
- *Many Negroes were taught to read and write. Many were allowed to meet in groups. They went visiting at night and owned guns… Most of them were treated with kindness.*
- *Male field hands received each year two summer suits, two winter suits, a straw hat, a wool hat, and two pairs of shoes.*
- *Taken from an Opinion Column by Dana Milbank of the Washington Post, February 1, 2022*

Someone should have shared this information with George Washington. The contents of this book are closer to standup comic material than historical facts. This is insane. It is my view, that the owner/overseer would have been shot minutes after enslaved persons acquired their first gun.

CHAPTER 22

The Christian church

'Everybody talking 'bout Heaven ain't going there...'
(taken from an old Negro Spiritual)

This chapter is about the role played and the harm caused by the Christian church while claiming to represent God. Consider the following true statements:

A. The Christian Church has been a force of good in this country and worldwide for centuries, building hospitals, global food programs, and responding to disasters

B. Agents of the Christian Church have globally caused great harm in the name of Christ for centuries

The Doctrines of Discovery resulted from several Papal Bulls - public decrees - written during the 15th century. The Vatican issued these public decrees, which claimed entitlements for certain groups because Christianity was superior to other cultures and religions. In 1493 Pope Alexander VI established Christian dominion over the

'New World'. The Pope issued these decrees after the Great Schism (the divide between Western Christianity and Eastern Christianity) of 1054, but before the Protestant Reformation Movement of the 16th century, which challenged the religious and political authority of the Catholic Church. Thus, in the 15th century, most Christians in the West recognized the authority and supremacy of the Pope. Thus, through this doctrine, the church granted Europeans the divine right to displace Indigenous, non-Christian people worldwide and take possession of their 'undiscovered' land by any means necessary. These public decrees also provided cover for the kidnapping and enslavement of Africans and the rights of the colonial settlers. This explains why some Christian Europeans came to this continent engrained with the view of White superiority or a sense of entitlement. Many came to this continent convinced they were entitled to both free land and labor.

The conquest and colonization of non-Christians sanctioned the brutal, inhumane treatment of Indigenous people in Africa, America, and other parts of the world. It was considered justified because these groups were 'enemies of Christ'.

I suggest that the Indigenous people never heard of Christ until introduced by those kidnapping them, murdering them, stealing their land, and looting their natural resources. These so-called Christians were not the best of witnesses. *Everybody talking 'bout heaven ain't going there.*

The Doctrine of Discovery was first articulated as a legal formulation in the United States Supreme Court case, Johnson v. M'Intosh, in 1823. This case defines international property law today and is used by companies and countries to extract natural resources from Indigenous people worldwide.

The Christian church's failure to be at the forefront of denouncing these actions, rather than encouraging them is the most egregious of the institution's shortcomings in my view. With the Christian church being on the wrong side of this issue, many fail to see the need for God in their lives. This negligence is a missed opportunity to point the world to Christ.

The Christian church should share the inspired message of God's redemptive work to the world, becoming a beacon of light piercing the darkness. Christ's work, completed at the cross, exemplifies God's unconditional love for all humanity. The distinguishing aspect of Christ's work should separate his followers from the rest of the world. All reflect the image of God; all have dignity; all have worth, and the story of redemption is for all men and women. In other words, All Lives Matter! Followers of Christ should proclaim and LIVE this good news to all.

While some Christian leaders have proclaimed the good news of Jesus Christ to the nation, other Christian leaders have offered different interpretations. False prophets were common in the days of the Old Testament and are among us today. False prophets during the Old Testament time told the King, and the people, what they wanted to hear, claiming it to be a word from God. People were then motivated by money, desire for fame, and access to power, just as people are today.

According to the wisest man who ever lived, "There is nothing new under the sun." A true prophet speaks truth to power and tells everyone within the sound of his voice, what "Thus said the Lord." A true prophet would have advised southern leaders prior to the Civil War that things would not end well. A true prophet would have informed the citizens they would exchange riches for poverty, abundance for scarcity, and vibrant cities for smoldering ruins.

In the Old Testament Book of I Kings, Chapter 22, the King of Israel (Ahab) contemplated war with the King of Syria. Ahab sought the council of 400 false prophets, all of whom prophesied an Ahab victory. However, the one true prophet informed the King the war would not end well. The King took the advice of the 400 false prophets and lost his life the following day.

During the civil rights struggle, a true prophet would have advised southern leaders that it was wrong to continue the disenfranchisement of people of color. They would have declared it was not right to have police officers on the public payroll wearing police uniforms during the day and KKK robes at night, burning and bombing Black homes and churches. A true prophet would have said it was not right to allow police officers to beat, use attack dogs, and fire hoses on protesters attempting to exercise their constitutional rights.

A true man, or woman, of God would have spoken up and said, such sinful behavior is displeasing to the Almighty.

A true prophet would have advised that a new day was coming and the old was making way for the new.

Many argue that slavery did not start in America, so what's the big deal. I agree slavery existed before Europeans came to these shores - the United States. However, so did the act of murder. Few would argue that murder was okay because it originated elsewhere.

In October 2021, Pastor Tony Evans of Texas posted a YouTube video, A Message to My White Friends, speaking to the faith family. The pastor stated that the White evangelical church in America endorsed a system of slavery, Jim Crow, and other ungodly deeds. This was because they refused to affirm the humanity of Africans living in America, thus providing cover for the culture. Pastor Evans further stated that Exodus 21:16 states the kidnapping and enslavement of a person is a capital offense. The punishment for such a crime is death. However, the American church chose to overlook 'inconvenient' Scripture passages.

I grew up in the Church of Christ Holiness USA, founded by a spirit-filled man, Bishop Charles P. Jones. Bishop Jones wrote several worship songs, including *There's a Happy Time A–Coming*, based on Malachi 4:1-2. The song celebrates the fact that the oppressor will not always be able to oppress. Many find this and other biblical teachings uncomfortable and unpleasant. However, to quote another of my former pastors,

Bishop Williams, "If you have a problem with this, don't complain to me, you take it up with God. It is in his book."

While many White preachers in the Bible Belt vehemently opposed the Civil Rights movement, true prophets were among them. One hundred years after the Civil War, Blacks were still terrorized daily. The Reverend Robert Graetz, who supported the 1955 Montgomery Bus Boycott, was a true prophet. The treatment Graetz received was similar to that of Old Testament prophets. According to the USA's September 20, 2020, online edition, 'Graetz was the only White clergyman to support the boycott. Like other participants, they persisted in the face of harassment, terrorism, and death threats that extended to their preschool children. Vandals poured sugar in their gas tank, and the family home was bombed twice.'

On September 30, 1962, a riot occurred due to an African American, James Meredith, being admitted to the previously segregated University of Mississippi. Shortly after, Pastor James B. Nicholson of the Byram Methodist Church told his members, "We have let prejudice shut out the Gospel and in many areas of our lives have turned to the gods of segregation and White supremacy to sustain us." This message was not well received.

Church members tried to replace Pastor Nicholson. When the district superintendent blocked the pastor's removal, members of the congregation boycotted church services. But Pastor Nicholson was a true prophet in the Old Testament mold. Nicholson and another 27 White Methodist pastors signed a Born of Conviction document published in the Mississippi Methodist Advocate on January 2, 1963. (God always has a remnant.) The signatories argued that discrimination was inconsistent with biblical principles. They also strongly condemned communism because those expressing empathy for the plight of African Americans were often labeled communists. I guess *because* only communists expressed concern for the *Least of These*.

The Born of Conviction document proved to be very unpopular in Mississippi. Pastor Nicholson and two other pastors lost their ministerial positions; while others received threats or were shunned by their congregations.

In 2 Timothy 4:2, Saint Paul urges Timothy, "Preach the word; in season, out of season, reprove, rebuke, exhort." In 2 Timothy 4:3, Paul advises Timothy that a time is coming when people "...will not endure sound doctrine... because they have itching ears... and will turn their ears away from the truth and be turned aside to fables."

I believe Paul is telling us to always look for opportunities to share God's word. If the message is unpopular, preach it anyway. Amid wrongdoing, one is to speak truth to power. But Paul also warns us that people will turn away from the truth because of their evil desires.

The position taken by the Born of Conviction document signatories may have been unpopular. Still, the pastors correctly interpreted God's Holy Word. The signatories were on the side of justice. Students of American history could make a strong argument the White church was on the wrong side of history regarding both slavery and the civil rights movement.

In my view, historians will come to the same conclusion regarding the White evangelical community's lack of support for the Black Lives Matter movement. While some attempt to turn back the clock, others press toward a more perfect union.

Several years before the Civil War, regional tensions erupted within the American Baptist Church. The northern branch was against the institution of slavery; the southern branch supported the kidnapping, enslavement, rape, murder, and continued mistreatment of the enslaved Africans. The bond holding the two eventually broke, and the southern branch became the Southern Baptist Convention.

One hundred years later, the racial attitudes of the Southern Baptist Convention mainly remain the same. In Sarah Posner's book, 'Unholy',

Posner reports the current evangelical political movement originated over desegregation concerns and not abortion, as most have come to believe. Posner states,

> "But as much as abortion is now, four decades later, the centerpiece of the religious right agenda, the real story of the formation of this movement was not about protecting babies, families, or morality. Instead, it was a story of racist backlash against school desegregation and other civil rights advances," page 100

Before the Roe v Wade judgment, the Reverend Jerry Falwell had a church, a television show (which often expressed racist views), and the Lynchburg Christian Academy.

The academy was one of many private schools formed, allowing White families to avoid sending their children to newly integrated public schools. Things changed in 1974 when the Internal Revenue Service revoked the tax-exempt status of segregated private schools under the Ford Administration. According to the Internal Revenue Service, segregation violated the Civil Rights Act of 1964.

Defense of racial segregation and not abortion spurred Falwell into political action. Aware that the tax status change would impact the school's financial health, the Reverend and like-minded White God-fearing, Bible-believing Christians jumped into action.

To be clear, these Christian leaders and their followers were at the forefront of retaining racial segregation and the continued disenfranchisement of people of color, including police brutality, violation of voting rights, and the continued economic exploitation of Black people.

Friends of the good Reverend Falwell claim the politically connected conservative Christian leader sprang into action over the Roe v. Wade judgment. Falwell supporters claim that the Reverend's sermons were nonpolitical before this egregious decision. In keeping with this story, while reading about this issue the day following this decision, Falwell was so disturbed he had to act. The legal wholesale slaughter of innocent babies was more than the good Reverend could stand.

As others do, Posner reports that Falwell waited at least three years after the Roe v. Wade judgment before addressing this issue consistently. Posner also exposes the myth that neither the evangelical movement nor the Reverend engaged in political actions before taking up the mantle against the Supreme Court's 1973 Roe v. Wade judgment.

Falwell was at the forefront of the campaign against civil rights years before the abortion fight. While the good Reverend may not have developed immediate strong feelings about abortions, he had instantaneous solid convictions about segregation and the disenfranchisement of African Americans. Falwell was 100% in favor of the status quo, and used his platform to share his views and opinions.

The Roe v. Wade judgment became the substitute issue used to attract voters to his cause of keeping the Black man in his place. Around the time of the Roe judgment, the continued disenfranchisement of Black people was falling out of vogue. Opposing the Roe judgment allowed Falwell to stake a questionable claim to the moral high ground while spouting his racist ideology of victimhood against Federal Government overreaches. This 'overreach' granted fair treatment to people of color.

My college professor once explained that when viewers watch a particular television show, the announcer would often state that the program is brought to them by a specific sponsor. The college professor further explained a more accurate statement would be that the program delivers the viewer to the sponsor. Beer companies do not advertise on Saturday morning cartoon shows. Sellers of children's breakfast cereal do not advertise on Monday Night Football Games. The Roe V. Wade judgment became the vehicle for gaining access to a broad base of people identifying as Christians and the umbrella covering his repugnant views.

It only takes a brief examination into Falwell's political ploy to expose apparent holes. Falwell is pro-life, except for Black life. While Black people in South Africa were dying at the hands of the White minority, the good Reverend Falwell opposed sanctions against the South African Government.

Before the beginning of the abortion movement, many Christians were not politically active, including members of the Southern Baptist Convention. The different factions of the Protestant Community were able to bridge their differences and join the Catholic Community in opposition to the Roe V. Wade issue. The groups bonded and became politically active. The Catholic Church had a long standing opposition to abortion but more moderate positions on others socials issues. Falwell and his allies absorbed their other grievances with the abortion issue and merged the groups. They folded the group into the Republican Party in the United States, becoming a powerful force within the Grand Old Party, the self-claimed party of family values.

This new alignment between White Christians and the Grand Old Party was a good fit. Other group members were unaware, unconcerned about, or agreed with Falwell's other issues. This pro-life political party accepts funds from the gun lobby and military hardware makers, resulting in an untold number of deaths each year. The political party claims pro-life status but spent years attempting to prevent and remove health care from millions of Americans. The Grand Old Party claims to be pro-family but constantly tries to eliminate family assistance programs and advocates slashing funding for the elderly.

Reverend Falwell utilized this newly expanded platform to promote his distasteful, unchristian, and unbiblical views. Falwell continued to give his full support to the segregation, disenfranchisement, official and unofficial acts of brutality towards African Americans at the behest of police, and various domestic terrorist groups like the KKK.

The *Civil Rights Act of 1964* outlawed discrimination based on race, color, religion, or national origin. The Act also enforces every citizen's right to vote, the cornerstone of a democratic society. This man of the cloth, Reverend Falwell, strongly opposed this legislation calling it a "... violation of human rights." He further suggested the bill resulted from communists and left-wing influences. Because I guess, only communists and left-leaning individuals support both democracy and Biblical principals not Christians.

If I understand Falwell's reasoning correctly, only communists and those with *left-leaning* political views also support the concept of fair treatment for all citizens. This was a weak argument, especially for those acquainted with biblical teaching, but it appeared to be strong enough for his *God-fearing* congregation. I suggest that a Bible teaching church would better serve these members. Furthermore, the community and the entire country would have been better served if this church had closed its doors.

To paraphrase Pastor Gerald Harris of Gilroy, California (Church of God in Christ), *you may go to jail if you get a bad lawyer. If you get the wrong doctor, you may not get well. If one listens to the wrong preacher, you might end up in hell.*

Reverend Falwell's stance speaks volumes about his ministry, church, and the organization he brazenly named the *Moral Majority*. One would never mistake Falwell for the *Good Samaritan*. In the parable known as the Good Samaritan, the main character has compassion for someone outside of his tribe. The parable provides a biblical definition of one's neighbor.

According to the parable, a certain man went down from Jerusalem to Jericho and fell among thieves. The man was stripped of his belongings, seriously injured, and left on the side of the road. Eventually, a priest - a religious man, came. Seeing the injured man clinging to life, he passed on the other side of the road, continuing his journey. Likewise, a Levite - a man with religious/temple responsibilities, also continued and passed on the other side of the road.

When a certain Samaritan - a man from a different country and despised by the Jewish people, came upon the injured man, the Samaritan had compassion for him. After attending to his injuries, the Samaritan set the man on his beast and took him to an inn. Upon reaching the inn, the Samaritan gave the innkeeper money for lodging, care, and provisions and said he would pay additional funds for the injured man's care upon his return.

Thus, the biblical definition of one's neighbor is anyone you meet needing help you can provide. One's neighbor is not limited to the people living next door, down the street or someone who shares one's skin tone.

On March 7, 1965, social justice warriors attempted a peaceful civil rights march from Selma, Alabama, to the state Capitol. Along the way, the protestors had to cross their own personal Jericho Road, *aka the Edmund Pettus Bridge*. This bridge was built in 1940, seventy-five years after the Civil War. The bridge honors the memory of Edmund Winston Pettus, a Confederate General, United States Senator, and Grand Dragon of the Alabama KKK.

The brutality against those seeking social justice on March 7, 1965, would have made Pettus proud. The group attacking the social warriors paid homage to the great General with the protesters' blood, sweat, and tears. Pettus and his fellow Confederate cohorts would have been most pleased indeed. The terrorists did not feel the need to hide behind sheets and hoods that day. The public opinion of southern Whites was on their side. The day became known as *Bloody Sunday*.

The social justice protesters encountered an army of police on horses with cattle prods, billy clubs, tear gas, and a heavily armed civilian mob. A cursory review of these scenes reveals social justice protesters peacefully exercising constitutional rights to which all Americans are entitled. At a certain point, the terrorists attacked the protestors. The uniformed police officers did not rush to aid the protesters but instead joined the mob.

The two groups - the terrorists and police, vied to see who could be the most vicious. The police and their posse friends assaulted men, women, and children. They inflicted many serious injuries, thus providing worldwide visual proof of the protesters' claims of mistreatment and civil rights violations. In the natural, it appeared the terrorists won the day. The march ended with wounded victims fleeing and others on the ground in desperate need of medical attention.

However, many believe the violence on *Bloody Sunday* led to a turning point in the Civil Rights Movement. The passing of the *Civil Rights Act of 1964* had outlawed discrimination based on race, color, religion, or national origin. The law also ensured every citizen's right to vote, which is the cornerstone of a democratic government. African Americans accounted for half of the population in Dallas County, Alabama yet only two percent of the registered voters were Black. The march drew attention to this fact. Reverend Falwell strongly opposed this legislation and claimed it violated human rights. So, according to Falwell, allowing all citizens the right to vote, and fair treatment was a human rights violation.

Falwell was able to look past the fog from the tear gas and blood and tears of the marchers and glean truths others missed. The good reverend did not hesitate to express his strong views on the protest march. The mob and police came to the bridge armed with weapons, which they were anxious to use, while the social justice warriors came with Bibles, praying and singing songs of Zion. Falwell claimed the communist-inspired agitators and protesters were responsible for the violence, thus speaking volumes about his character or lack thereof. (To the best of my knowledge, communists generally do not go around carrying Bibles and singing hymns.)

In addition, Falwell insinuated that Dr. King, the one without the weapons, was a lying communist and questioned Dr. King's commitment to non-violence.

One of the two was lying, and I do not believe it was Dr. King.

Dr. King was the victim of illegal arrests, the bombing of his home, beating, stabbing, and eventually losing his life to an assassin's bullet. I am unaware of Dr. King ever engaging in violence, even when others committed violence against him.

In my opinion, Dr. King sincerely believed in his non-violence philosophy.

Reverend Falwell failed to see a contradiction between being a Christian and supporting segregation, Jim Crow, or the mistreatment of marginalized members of society. In other words, 'the least these'.

So, here is a *man of the cloth* siding with the oppressors instead of the oppressed and blaming the oppressed for protesting the oppressed status they entered at birth.

It is not difficult to guess how Reverend Falwell would have responded had he been on the road to Jericho that day. He may well have kicked the guy before crossing the road - without offering help.

The late Reverend Falwell's supporters suggest the preacher was focused on spreading the good news of *Jesus Christ* and less concerned about social or political issues. However, this narrative is inconsistent with available facts.

In 1968, Reverend Falwell invited third-party presidential candidate George Wallace - considered by many to be a lunatic, running as a segregationist to speak at his church. Wallace rose to international notoriety due to his hostility toward African Americans while serving as governor. (The governor famously said, "Segregation today... segregation tomorrow... segregation forever.") This invitation to segregationists shed volumes of light on Falwell's political views. In later years, the governor modified his political philosophy and attracted a degree of support from the African American community.

Reverend Falwell was not the only Bible-thumping, scripture quoting preacher to oppose the Civil Rights movement. Most of his peers stood in agreement with this stance. Some suggested that God was only interested in the *hereafter*, not the *here and now*. However, the invitation to the segregationist presidential candidate, George Wallace, indicated the late preacher was very much concerned about the *here and now*.

All followers of Christ should agree on certain biblical principles, such as the *Great Commission*. However, I believe that sharing the word of God while ignoring the living conditions of those on the receiving end of the message, is inconsistent with biblical teaching.

James 2:15-16 says, "If a brother or sister is naked and destitute of daily food, and one of you say to them be warmed and filled, but you do not give them the things which are needed for the body, what does it profit?"

I believe the writer is saying that merely expressing the doctrine of faith is not enough. Such actions fall short. The Christian life should transform our conduct, acts, and thoughts.

The social justice protesters demonstrated against obstacles preventing citizens from exercising their constitutional rights. Rights that Reverend Falwell opposed. By sharing his platform with the governor, Falwell endorsed these obstacles. Many non-believers view these actions, endorsing segregation, and Jim Crow with disdain. Thus, Falwell and his cohorts caused significant harm to the *Body of Christ* and impeded the *Great Commission* with these actions.

Elements of the American Christian Church continue to provide cover, approval, validity, and justification for a system that degrades groups of people and violates the Constitution of the United States. This began for Africans in 1619, before the country's foundation and continues to this day.

Among the Black Codes enacted in the southern states after the Civil War was a law making it illegal for a Black person to be unemployed. *Unemployment in the African American community often trends higher than in other communities.* The punishment for unemployment was imprisonment. As a prisoner, they became available for leasing to White farmers at low rates. The former enslaved person went from being *owned* to being *rented*, again providing labor without compensation. These laws and similar codes failed to receive significant pushback from Christians.

Dr. Robert P. Jones offers insight into why the Christian church did not speak out against this oppression in his book, 'White Too Long'. Dr Jones opens his book with the following: "The Christian denomination in which I grew up was founded on the proposition that chattel slavery could flourish alongside the Gospel of Jesus Christ. Its founders believed this arrangement was not just possible, but also divinely mandated."

Dr Robert P. Jones grew up in a Southern Baptist Church, was baptized at age six, and attended church services several nights a week. His religious instruction included Southern Baptist denominational policy and doctrine classes. However, Jones did not learn about the Southern Baptist Convention's White supremacist roots until he was a seminary student in graduate school. Jones also stated:

> "While the South lost the War, this secessionist religion
> not only survived but also thrived. Its powerful role as
> a religious institution that sacralized White supremacy
> allowed the Southern Baptist Convention to spread
> its roots during the late 19th century to dominate
> southern culture. And by the mid-20th century, the
> Southern Baptist Convention ultimately evolved into the

single largest Christian denomination in the country, setting the tone for American Christianity overall and Christianity's influence in public life." page 2

This influence continues and explains the solid evangelical support for a former President of the United States who also enjoyed strong support from White supremacy groups from all over the country. An uncomfortable fact is the two groups are often the same. Much like Reverend Jerry Falwell, many Christian leaders advocate White supremacy today.

Dr. Robert P. Jones' book also documents the fact that nonreligious Whites have more empathy toward social justice issues than whose who identify as evangelicals.

During the summer of 2020, a megachurch pastor in the Western part of the country discussed the *Black Lives Matter* movement with his congregation. The good pastor screamed, "*Black Lives Matter* movement is from the devil. It is from Satan himself."

This is a far heavier rap to overcome than mere communism.

To prove his point, the *man of God* read from a document claiming to be from the *Black Lives Matter* movement, expressing support for the LGBTQ community. That was the sum of his proof. The *Black Lives Matter* movement was from the devil because it articulated empathy and compassion for a fellow marginalized group. This preacher was a strong supporter of a former president of the United States who enjoyed support from conspiracy theorists. This *man of God* also prophesied that voters would re-elect the president, which did not happen.

As previously noted, this preacher's position is not unique. Dr. Bob Jones, an evangelist, religious broadcaster, founder, and first president of Bob Jones University, intensely opposed the civil rights struggle. According to published reports, Dr. Bob Jones famously stated, "If you oppose segregation, you oppose God." This is a twisted, convoluted gospel version designed to support and propagate hate-filled White supremacy views.

To be clear, the Southern Baptist Convention opposed the abolitionist movement before the Civil War. After the war, the Southern Baptist Convention strongly opposed Reconstruction and the granting of progressive policies such as voting rights to the newly freed enslaved people. The Southern Baptist Convention opposed financial compensation for the formerly enslaved while supporting oppressive, inhuman Jim Crow laws that replaced Reconstruction. This Christian body opposed every progressive organization, social movement, and legislation between the Civil War and the Civil Rights Movement. This included furthering social progress, such as labor laws, child labor protections, voting rights, women's rights, and civil rights for all marginalized Americans, including the formerly enslaved.

Rather than integrating the public schools as required by law, these *Christians* violated the law. They formed private *Christian* schools, financed in part by their tax-exempt status, that did not accept non-White students. When faced with the loss of tax-exempt status due to their discriminatory practices, they claimed to be the real victims and not those who endured both enslavement and Jim Crow.

So, the White Christians claimed victimization because they could no longer enjoy tax-exempt status while violating the law. They claimed to be the real victims instead of the groups currently experiencing marginalization, economic exploitation, mob violence, and police brutality. The White Christians were mistreated and not those having to navigate Sundown towns and endure lynching and massacres. *Sundown towns acquired this name from posted signs advising people of color to leave town before sundown or face unspeakable violence.*

These racist Christians appealed their case to the United States Supreme Court, which ruled against their claim by eight-to-one. *The Justice who voted in their favor was later appointed Chief Justice.* This same group of Christians firmly opposed the *Black Lives Matter* movement often claiming that the *Black Lives Matter* protestors are the ones who are racist.

According to Nathalie Baptiste, writing for Mother Jones Magazine, dated 3/29/2021:

"Wokeness becomes synonymous with oppression itself. Black Lives Matter spun into Blue Lives Matter. 'I can't breathe' is adopted by antimaskers as their smirking slogan. The mantras and catchwords of movements that challenge the status quo are co-opted by reactionaries who want to quash those efforts. They've flipped on their head, turned inside out, repurposed to sneer at the people they were meant to rally, and generally made to seem comical and ridiculous – a rhetorical minstrel act. Essentially, the theme is the old American standby that there's no greater racist than the anti-racist, no greatest tyrant than the slave who wants to be free. Republicans refer to Black people calling out injustice as a 'woke mob'. Perhaps no phrase had undergone this type of distortion more prominently than the phrase 'Black Lives Matter'. After shooting and killing 17-year-old Trayvon Martin in Florida the year before, activists Patrisse Cullors, Alicia Garza, and Opal came up with the rallying cry. It wasn't long before protesters began chanting, "Black Lives Matter" and holding up 'Black Lives Matter' signs at protests for the endless list of Blacks cut short by violence. Racist Whites quickly came up with a retort: "All lives matter." As Black Lives Matter was met with 'all lives' matter and 'blue lives matter', it became increasingly clear that these phrases weren't really about equality or even about law enforcement, as demonstrated by the January 6 Capitol siege in which insurrectionists assaulted cops with pro-police flags. They were about reminding Black people of their place in society."

Many biblical scholars believe Jesus was a Jewish Middle Eastern refugee with brown skin. Many White evangelicals often express hostility toward refugees and people with darker skin. In Galatians 3:28, Apostle Paul writes, "there is no difference between Jew and Greek, slave and free person, male and female. You are all the same in Christ Jesus."

Yet, many who identify as evangelical appear unaware of Saint Paul's teaching.

Social media posts from evangelicals often support building a wall on the country's southern border (but not the northern border) to impede border crossing by certain groups. They often claim, "This is our country and we have the right to keep certain people out." However, Psalms 24:1 reads, "The earth is the Lord's, and the fulness thereof: the world, and they that dwell therein." In other words, the earth and the people living on the earth belong to Him. It is not ours, it does not belong to us, but to the Creator.

In June 1995, during the 150th Anniversary of the Southern Baptist Convention, a resolution was presented to convention delegates. The resolution acknowledged this organization's role in defending slavery and condoning systemic racism and apologizes to the African American community for these actions. The Southern Baptist Convention eventually passed the resolution after overcoming fierce opposition.

Some delegates suggested that current members of the Southern Baptist Convention had not enslaved anyone - their forefathers had - thus, apologies were unnecessary. However, in the ninth chapter of the

Book of Daniel, the Prophet confesses his forefathers' sins and asks for God's mercy.

In Revelation 7:9, St John wrote, "...I looked and behold, a great multitude that no man could number, from every nation, from all tribes, and people and languages, standing before the throne and before the Lamb..." To clarify, I believe the author says that people from all over the world will worship together in paradise. People from different political parties will worship alongside one another.

Although the merger between certain church groups and the Republican Party appeared profitable, some suggest such a union can damage the Body of Christ. Nilay Saniya's article in the May 6, 2021, edition of *Christianity Today Magazine*, stated when church leaders promote a particular political party or seek the attention of political leaders, the church suffers. According to Saniya, Christianity is growing faster in Asia than the countries' population. More than 700 million Christians are on the African continent where Christianity lacks governmental support.

Associating the Christian faith with a specific government or political party can cause people to turn from the church. This happens when they view the faith as supporting policies that they find morally untenable, such as religious intolerance, bigotry, police brutality, and hostility toward women, refugees, etc.

History suggests that church growth often occurs during periods of persecution and oppression. That is when there are arrests, assaults, and imprisonment, to people associated with a particular faith. This does not include the phony culture wars, such as the war on Christmas. Fake wars restrict the number of people receptive to hearing about the mercy of God, the grace of God, or the goodness of God. Most people continue to say Merry Christmas and do not know of anyone forced to do otherwise. Those interested in grooming favor with political leaders run the risk of becoming distracted from God's will and are often more concerned about maintaining access to those in power.

Suppose you believe, as some do, that the message of the Gospel is a message of violence, fear, hate, contempt for the poor, lack of concern for the sick, full of anger, resentment, COVID deniers, negativity, and wild conspiracies, then I urge you to read the words of Christ for yourself. You can find his words primarily in the New Testament Books of Matthew, Mark, Luke, and John. You will find that Christ does not advocate hate but preaches love. He does not promote violence nor fear of refugees. He expresses compassion for the sick, the poor, and marginalized groups. Jesus offers comfort to the oppressed and admonishes the oppressors. In the Gospels, you will find a God of mercy, a God of grace, and a God of love. I strongly suggest you ignore the rhetoric surrounding Christian nationalism and find a true community of faith. A community of genuine worshipers who rightly proclaim the word of God.

POSTSCRIPT:

The Christian faith is more than just rhetoric. The Christian faith entails a life of actions and of deeds. It may require one to sail against the wind, taking a position contrary to popular opinion or against most of one's tribe. God is not calling for culture Christians. One must be fully engaged and wholly embrace the teaching of Christ. We must also study God's word for ourselves. By doing so, we will be able to recognize the questionable teachings of others. Proverbs 29:7 says, "The righteous considers the cause of the poor, but the wicked does not understand such knowledge."

CHAPTER 23

The Least of These

*T**his section examines the fate that befalls those who mistreat or fail to address the needs of "the least of these."*

Then they will also answer him, saying,

> "Lord, when did we see You hungry or thirsty or a stranger or naked or sick or in prison and did not minister to You?"

Then he will answer them saying,

> "Assuredly, I say unto you, in as much as you did not do it to one of the *Least of These*, you did not do it to Me. And these will go away into everlasting punishment but the righteous into eternal life."

Matthew 25:44-46.

He may say to some: "I was a stranger/refugee. I arrived at your southern border after fleeing my home country in search of a safe harbor. You did not let me in. You separated me from my children, locked them in cages, and sent me back to a life of peril."

Someone else may hear: "I was among the sharecroppers during the Jim Crow era, and you cheated me year after year. When I questioned your figures, you called the sheriff who beat me bloody and threw me in jail." *Disclosure: my grandparents were sharecroppers; my great grandparents were enslaved.*

He may tell someone else: "I was sick and could not afford my medication. Other countries sold the drug I needed for a few dollars. But in your position, you conspired to keep prices much higher for personal gain."

Someone else may hear: "I was in desperate need of healthcare. As a public official, you denied healthcare expansion to my area for political reasons. You said it was due to the lack of public funds, but you had no problem lowering taxes and granting other favors to the wealthy."

You may ask, what is this *everlasting punishment*? In the story of the Rich Man and Lazarus (Luke 16:19-31), Jesus offers us insight into this question.

A certain rich man wore expensive clothing and ate each day lavishly. There is also a beggar in this story, named Lazarus, full of sores, who lay at the rich man's gate, hoping for the crumbs that fall from the rich man's table. Dogs would come and lick the sores that covered the beggar's body. In a manner of speaking, the beggar was *one of the Least of These.*

One day, the beggar died and was carried to Abraham's bosom by the angels. The rich man died, was buried, went to Hades, and suffered greatly. Amid his suffering, the rich man saw both Abraham and Lazarus in the distance. The rich man cried out, "Father Abraham, have mercy on me, and send Lazarus that he may dip the tip of his finger in water and cool my tongue; for I am tormented in this flame (Luke 16:24)." His agony was so great, that he longed for the relief a single drop of water might bring.

But in response to the rich man's request, Abraham said, 'Son, remember...' (Luke 16:25a).

I believe we will remember a lot of things in the hereafter.

The creator of the universe illustrates in the above passage what one can expect in this place of torment after this life. It is a place to avoid at all costs.

In the next life, we will be conscious. We will be aware of our surroundings. We will see, feel, talk, recognize others, and remember the past. We will remember things we did that we regret doing and think of things we did not do that we should have done. In this place of torment, there will be much reflecting.

Extending the hand of biblical friendship to marginalized people is not in vogue. Today's culture celebrates mean-spiritedness, harsh language, and even harsher deeds.

Lazarus was a member of the marginal group and was among the *Least of These*. The rich man knew Lazarus was often hungry but never sent a plate of food or extended an invitation for a meal. The rich man was aware Lazarus required medical attention but offered no assistance. Lazarus was a 'beggar,' which suggests he was impoverished and perhaps in need of shelter. The rich man with more than he could use, offered the poor man nothing.

The Bible is clear. Those who ignore the *Least of These* or mistreat them in this life risk hearing 'on that day of days,' the most dreadful of words in any language as recorded in the 25th Chapter of Matthew,

Depart from me... I never knew you...

Reflections

A church is not a building, but rather a group of people - its members. In theory, a church encourages and teaches the gospel message, the good news of Jesus Christ. The Christian Church should encourage its members to embrace Christ's teaching and become 'both hearers and doers of his word.' The congregation learns of God's mercy, His grace, and His love. All are entitled to dignity. However as noted, not all 'Christian Churches' embrace the teachings of Christ; some have different agendas.

Some churches promote a misguided 'Christian theology' (based on tribal passions not Biblical principles), These groups inflicted long lasting damage creating intergenerational traumas to Indigenous people globally. Many of these traumas continue to exist. People claiming to represent the church actively worked to deprive people of their humanity and their culture identity while looting their natural resources.

Where do your church members stand?

Does your church promote cultural Christianity or Biblical teaching?

Regarding those experiencing food and other basic insecurities; does your church support feeding the hungry, clothing the naked, or do they suggest that those lacking food shelter, and clothes should just work harder? Does your church oppose government programs designed to help those in need equating such help as socialism?

Regarding strangers aka refugees - Does your church welcome refugees fleeing for their lives with programs to assist in assimilating? Or do they advocate erecting a wall on the southern border, the northern border, or both borders?

Does your church openly identify with a particular political party regardless of their positions or the character of the party's leaders?

Does your church claim to support 'pro-life' but oppose government programs designed to provide children with a reasonable chance of a successful life beginning; programs such as job training for their parents, childcare, free school lunches, etc?

Does your church oppose the teaching of historical events in public schools that some find 'uncomfortable'? Does your church believe the classroom should be a 'fact free' environment and promote false narratives aka lies?

Do your fellow church members equate affordable health care with socialism, or believe in caring for the sick and that all should have quality health care?

Does your church teach forgiveness and advocate extending the hand of fellowship to parolees? Does your church have a prison ministry, or do they support the philosophy of 'lock them up and throw away the key'?

Does your church acknowledge systemic racism? Or do they believe, as do many evangelicals, that the country does not have a racist past and racism is not a problem now?

Does your church express empathy or compassion for the marginalized among us? Some Christian churches believe that expressing empathy for the marginalized is sinful. Per research conducted by Dr. Robert P. Jones as documented in his book, 'White Too Long,' (page 162) sixty-two percent of white Christians disagree with the following statement: 'Generations of slavery and discrimination have created conditions that make it difficult for blacks to work their way out of the lower class.'

It breaks down as follows:

67% of White evangelicals disagree with the statement
62% of White mainline Protestants disagree with the statement
57% of White Catholics disagree with this statement
40% of religiously unaffiliated Whites disagree with this statement
30% of African American Protestants disagree with this statement

Other research also suggests that religious unaffiliated Whites have more empathy for historically marginalized members of society than do their religiously affiliated counterparts. In fact, some Christian groups teach against empathy for the marginalized suggesting such activity is sinful (Holy Post Podcast #472).

Where do your fellow church members stand on these issues? Do they attempt to empower, or do they appear to lack empathy for 'the least of these'? Hebrews 13:2-3 encourages the reader to extend hospitality to strangers, "for some have entertained angels unawares. Remember those who are in prison as though in prison with them, and those who are mistreated…"

It is imperative to adhere to the teachings of Jesus Christ and attend a Bible-believing church. To paraphrase my friend Pastor Gerald Harris:

If you get the wrong lawyer, you may go to jail.

If you get the wrong doctor, you may not get well.

And if you listen to the wrong Preacher, you may one day find yourself in Hell.

If you have a problem with this (Christ's teachings on 'The Least of These,') don't waste your time going around here talking about me, "you go talk to God. It's in His Book. He put it there." *Paraphasing late Bishop A.D. Williams*

Acknowledgments

I have quoted from several sources in this book, including the following:

Anderson, Carol, *White Rage*, page 11, citing David B Davis, *The Rocky Road to Freedom – Crucial Barriers to Abolition in the Antebellum Years in the Promise of Liberty*, ed. Tsesis, xiii.

bloomberg.com August 25, 2021
Christianity Today May 6, 2021
Evans, Tony YouTube video January 2, 2021
history.com
Holy Bible
Jones, Robert P., *White Too Long*
Kanas City Star
Little, Becky *How Woodrow Wilson Tried to Reverse Black American Progress*
Mississippi Methodist Advocate
Mother Jones Magazine - March 29, 2021
Posner, Sarah, *Unholy*
San Jose Mercury
USA Today
Vox -YouTube October 12, 2020
Washington Post online edition November 19, 2018

Suggested reading

Alexander, Michelle, The New Jim Crow

Balmer, Randall, Bad Faith - Race and the Rise of the Religious Right

Loewen, James W. Sundown Towns

Mitchell, Jerry, Race Against Time A reporter Reopens the Unsolved Murder Cases of the Civil Rights Era

Schiess, Kaitlyn, The Liturgy of Politics

Stevens, Stuart, It Was All a Lie How the Republican Party Became Donald Trump

Stevenson. Bryan, Just Mercy

Recommended Podcasts

Holy Post w/ Phil Visher

Filled to the Brim w/ Dr. Lynn Willis

A special thanks to:

The Ark House Family for their interest, assistance and partnership in putting my thoughts on this subject in print.

My friend and mentor Andrew Jobling who provided help and encouragement at each step of this process, along with my fellow Elite Club/Open Forum Members:

Karen Guest for her expert counsel

Sandra Cagle for all of her assistance

Antoine and family for all that you do

My extended Family members

Pastor Ernest Henderson

Dr. David Willis

Annette Gatejen

Raymond and Loretta Thomas

Bishop Robert Winn

Pastor Gerald Harris

Joseph Winn

Vie Winn

And of course, to my wife, Judy

www.ingramcontent.com/pod-product-compliance
Lightning Source LLC
Chambersburg PA
CBHW071155260626
47162CB00003B/1058